Not Quite The Enemy

Nora Kane

Not Quite The Enemy

Lindsay Lane FBI Thriller

Nora Kane

Copyright © 2024 Nora Kane

All rights reserved. No portion of this publication may be reproduced, distributed, or transmitted in any form or by any means, including photocopying, recording, or other electronic or mechanical methods, without written permission from the publisher or author, except as permitted by U.S. copyright law. It is illegal to copy this book, post it to a website, or distribute it by any other means without written permission. This book is a work of fiction. Any reference to real people or real locales is used fictitiously. Other names, characters, places, and incidents are the product of the author's imagination, and any resemblance to actual events or locales or persons living or dead, is entirely coincidental.

ISBN: 9798342264600

Books by Nora Kane

Margot Harris Series One

Margot Harris Series Two

Margot Harris Series Three

Margot Harris Series Four

Margot Harris Series Five

Jade Pearson Mystery Series

Nora Kane's Full Library

Lindsay

"What do you have?" Willis, the square-jawed commander of the Hostage Rescue Team, asked. HRT is the FBI's version of a military Special forces team focused on domestic law enforcement.

He directed the question to Agent Smythe even though Lindsay was the one spearheading the investigation. If Willis noticed Special Agent Lindsay Lane standing next to Smythe, he didn't acknowledge it.

Smythe motioned to Lindsay.

Willis was still looking at Smythe when Lindsay said, "Pretty sure it was all in the reports."

"I like to hear it in person. Reading an email doesn't give me the same feel as hearing someone tell it."

Lindsay nodded; she didn't disagree. "Dennis Crumbly. Another anti-government militia type with a soft spot for Neo-Nazis. He made some like-minded friends and started having meetings both in person and online."

"Nothing illegal about that."

"No, there's not. Nothing illegal about buying a bunch of guns and enough ammunition to kill a small town twice either, which he's been doing. The illegal part is the bomb-making materials he's been buying in large quantities."

Willis nodded. He didn't seem so skeptical anymore.

"We've been monitoring him online. He's smart enough not to say anything blatantly incriminating but dumb enough to hint he has some big plans."

"Big plans could mean a lot of things."

"It could. Maybe he's just going to have a barbecue, but I doubt it. He never asked me to bring the potato salad."

"Why would he ask you?"

"She's been sitting in on their Zoom meetings," Smythe told him.

"They let women do that?"

"Women do a lot of things these days," Lindsay replied pointedly.

"Sure, but these guys tend to be extremely patriarchal. I'm not familiar with Crumbly's particular crowd, but if he's like the rest of them, there's not a lot of females sitting in on planning sessions."

"He's probably worse than most when it comes to that. I told them I didn't want to show my face in case the Feds were watching."

Smythe laughed. "Which they most definitely were."

Willis almost cracked a smile. "Why take the chance? Why not have someone who looked more the part do it?"

Lindsay shrugged. "I had an opportunity, and I seized it. If I'd waited for someone who looked the part to show up, who knows what might have happened? Besides, being paranoid about being identified helped me fit in."

"More people started hiding their faces and even using voice modulators after that," Smythe explained. "It was almost like they were trying to out-paranoid each other."

"Not that it mattered. They used the same IP addresses, and we knew who everyone was by then, for the most part."

"The most part?"

"One guy we never identified. Hopefully Crumbly can tell us who he is before we find out the hard way."

Willis nodded. "What kind of resistance should we expect?"

"The plan is to take him leaving work before he gets to his car, so probably light, though I wouldn't be surprised if he's carrying. The Stop and Shop doesn't allow their employees to conceal carry. Crumbly was very upset about that policy, but breaking the rules in the name of freedom is kind of Crumbly's thing."

"It's the American way. You said, 'before he got to the car'. That mean he's got weapons in there?"

"Likely a small arsenal. It'd be better not to let him get there."

"Thanks, I would have never thought of that." Willis's voice was dripping with sarcasm.

"Hey," Lindsay said, "you wanted to hear me say it, so I'm saying it."

"Fair point."

"Another team is hitting the house the second we take him into custody. He's bragged about contingency plans if the Feds show up at his place."

"Booby-trapped?"

"Possibly, but that won't be our concern. We're going to make sure he's in custody and not creating a situation when they hit the house. He'd love for us to make him famous."

"Even if all his fame comes post existing at room temperature."

"He'd prefer to be around for it, but I wouldn't put it past him. He likes the attention. He wants people to know he's a badass soldier of the cause. If he didn't, he might have flown right under our radar. If we give him a chance to make this a standoff, he's going to jump at it."

Willis agreed. "Okay, seems straightforward. You two going to wait here?"

Lindsay shook her head. "I'd kind of like to be there."

"This isn't like sitting behind a computer pretending to be sympathetic to the cause."

"Thanks, I would have never thought of that."

"She's tougher than she looks," Smythe added.

Willis focused on Smythe. "Maybe I was worried about you."

Smythe laughed. Willis didn't.

"Are you sure you wouldn't rather serve the warrant at the house?"

"To whom?" Lindsay asked. "Crumbly lives alone. Besides, the crime scene crew is better at searching his property than we are. I'd just be in the way."

"So, you'd rather be in my way?"

"I put a lot of time and effort into this. I want to be there when we take him down."

"You have a point," Willis agreed reluctantly. "Once we head that way, though, I'm in charge. If things go smooth I'll let you slap the bracelets on him yourself."

"Sounds good to me."

"If they don't..."

"It's your show."

Willis looked at the thick black watch on his wrist. "You can ride with me. My people should be getting into position as we speak."

Lindsay and Smythe left the makeshift field office on the outskirts of the small Colorado town and followed Willis to his Jeep Cherokee.

They were just about to climb in when Lindsay's phone buzzed. She checked it and saw a text from Special Agent Logan.

It read: *Good luck.*

Lindsay texted back: *Thanks.*

He replied: *Celebrate after?* and she answered with a thumbs-up emoji.

"What's that about?" Willis asked.

"Just a fellow agent wishing me luck," Lindsay replied.

Smythe smiled and shook his head. He was aware Logan and Lindsay's relationship was more than professional. He never said much about it, but it was clear he didn't think it was a good idea.

Lindsay gave him a piercing glance to cut off any smart-ass comments that might get Willis thinking she and Logan were more to each other than fellow agents. Logan and Lindsay felt it was best for both to keep their relationship private.

Once they were on the road, Willis turned to Lindsay. "How long have you been doing this, Agent Lane?"

"Long enough."

"Don't get touchy. I'm just asking because you don't appear to be that old."

"Thanks."

"It wasn't a compliment."

In the back seat, Smythe laughed.

"They recruit you out of college?"

"Yeah."

"I thought so."

"I suppose that wasn't a compliment either?"

"The college must have worked. You're a sharp one."

"You join after the army?"

"Marines."

"I can see it."

"Let me guess, that wasn't a compliment."

Lindsay shrugged. "It wasn't an insult."

Willis parked the Jeep across the street from the Stop and Shop where Crumbly was a clerk on the overnight shift. The sun was just coming up, signaling the end of his shift.

Willis put a headset on and started checking in with his people. An old van pulled up to the pumps and a dude dressed like a local, with blue jeans, a flannel shirt, a trucker-style baseball cap, and plenty of facial hair, got out and started filling the tank while another passenger dressed the same way got out and acted as if he was stretching his legs.

It was obvious to Lindsay that these men were part of the HRT. Both had firearms and Kevlar under their flannel shirts that were too new and clean to be worn by the locals. There were surely others lurking about, but Lindsay couldn't see any of them. According to the replies on Willis's headset, they were all out there and ready to go.

"I've got a pair of Kevlar vests under the seat," Willis said. "We won't be moving until after he's taken down but put them on anyway."

Smythe retrieved them and handed one to Lindsay.

"You always keep a few bulletproof vests under the passenger seat?" Smythe asked.

"No, they're usually in the trunk, but I figured you two would want to be here."

Lindsay and Smythe put on their vests over their clothing and then got low to watch the front door of the Stop and Shop.

"He should come out any second," Lindsay said.

"Good, my people can't pump gas forever."

A car pulled up and parked on the side of the building next to Crumbly's truck.

"That's Crumbly's replacement," Lindsay said. "If the pattern holds true, she'll go in, and he'll come right out."

They watched a middle-aged woman make her way to the front door. She didn't seem to be in any hurry. She walked inside and everyone in Willis's Jeep put one hand on their side arm and the other on their door handle.

The door opened and everybody tensed up, but instead of Crumbly, a teenage girl walked out. Rather than walking into the parking lot, she stopped by the door and dug a cigarette out of her purse.

She was dressed much like the FBI agents by the gas pumps. Her hair was cropped short and when she turned toward Willis's Jeep the multiple piercings on her face became visible. The sleeves on her shirt were rolled up to show off a few bad tattoos that could have meant she was older than she looked.

"Who's that?" Willis asked.

Lindsay said, "A customer?" as she picked up a pair of binoculars on the seat.

She focused on the girl but saw nothing up close that helped determine who she was.

"My people have been watching. They would have noticed a customer," Willis said as Lindsay focused on the tattoos to see if they gave away any gang affiliations.

She had a tattoo on her inner forearm, two arrows crossed over a skull in a circle of barbed wire. That could have been a gang symbol, but Lindsay didn't recognize it. While it could mark her as a gang member, it was just as likely the unfamiliar symbol was just a design that looked cool to the girl.

"As per our intel, Crumbly doesn't have a daughter or a girlfriend," Lindsay said as she lowered the binoculars. "She has to be a customer."

"She opened a brand-new pack of cigarettes," Smythe said. "I'd guess she just bought them."

"Customer or not, this could be a problem. I don't see a car in the lot."

"She must have walked."

Into the headset, Willis said, "Remember, take him on the side of the building before he gets to his car."

Before any of the HRT could reply, the door opened and Crumbly walked out. He was a big guy, though much of his bulk was around his mid-section. He towered over the girl. Instead of going straight to his late-model pickup truck off to the side of the building, he stopped to talk to her.

"Stand down," Willis said into his headset.

No one made a move. Crumbly kept talking to the girl.

"They seem to know each other," Willis said.

Lindsay and Smythe noticed the same thing.

"Could be a regular customer or perhaps a friend's kid?" Smythe said.

"Or a hostile," Willis said.

"I never noticed any teenage girls at any of the meetings," Lindsay replied.

"And they never noticed an FBI agent."

Lindsay thought Willis might have a point, but she didn't say so.

The discussion appeared to become heated. Crumbly's body language seemed angry. He was making a face and shaking his head. The young girl said something and then made a show of smoking her cigarette. She blew smoke up toward his face. Between his height and the wind, he didn't get much smoke in his face, but the fact she tried still pissed him off.

Crumbly pulled back his arm as if he was going to hit her. She acted as if he wasn't there. This seemed to piss him off even more.

"For a random customer, she sure knows how to push his buttons," Smythe said.

Crumbly lowered his arm but then raised it again. This time he made a fist.

"We going to let him do that?" Lindsay asked.

"Maybe she has it coming," Willis replied.

"That wasn't funny."

"I wasn't joking."

Crumbly lowered his arm without striking the kid. He said something and then started walking toward his truck.

"Get ready," Willis told his people.

Crumbly stopped about halfway. He looked back at the kid. He spoke loud enough that they could hear him say to her, "You coming or what?"

She smoked for a few seconds and acted as if she didn't hear him. He was beginning to say something else when she moved to join him.

"Kid or not, if Crumbly gets in the car, we might have a problem," Lindsay said.

She expected a sarcastic response, but Willis just nodded and said into the headset, "On my signal."

Crumbly stopped before he reached the corner of the store. He retrieved his phone and looked at the screen.

"What the fuck?" he said, loudly enough for everyone to hear.

"Take him down," Willis said. He could tell something was wrong. Lindsay and Smythe felt it too.

Crumbly looked over at the van and seemed to register movement. It was clear their cover was blown. He drew a gun from behind his back, a big chrome Colt Python .357, as he pulled the girl in front of him.

Willis left the Jeep. Lindsay and Smythe followed him.

The agents by the van drew their guns, HK sub-machine guns they had been carrying in shoulder rigs under their shirts. While they took aim, two more HRT members came out of the van. Unlike the two men pumping gas, they were in full tactical gear, having no reason to pretend they weren't HRT.

Crumbly put the gun to the girl's head and thumbed back the hammer.

"Stay back!" he screamed.

The agents in front of him did as they were told. The pair of men coming around on each side of the Stop and Shop stopped as well but not before putting Crumbly in their sights.

"What the hell are you doing?" the girl said as he held her tight.

"Shut up," he told her.

"Let me go, you fucking idiot," she yelled as she tried to pull away.

"Be still," Crumbly told her. To agents he said, "Stay back."

"You're going to get me killed," the girl said as she continued to struggle.

The look on Crumbly's face suggested he didn't mean to pull the trigger, but whether it was intentional or not, the gun fired and removed the top half of the young hostage's head.

He wiped her blood and brains from his face with the sleeve of his gun hand before he looked at her dead body and said, "Oh shit, I'm sorry."

Every gun from the FBI's HRT made those his last words as all eight men opened fire. The first bullet was enough, but he took seven more anyway. Each would have been fatal if he weren't already dead.

Willis looked at the two dead bodies on the sidewalk. "What the hell just happened?"

The closest man moved to the body. He picked up Crumbly's phone and looked at the face.

"Someone saw the raid on his house and tipped him off," he said to Willis. "They moved too soon."

Willis turned to Lindsay. "They were supposed to wait for us to confirm we had Crumbly."

"I know," she replied, seeing his rage directed at her. She added, "I didn't tell them to move."

Willis pointed to the dead girl. "She's just a kid. I have a niece her age."

Lindsay had nothing to say to that.

"You were the intelligence on this. How did you not know about her?"

Lindsay had nothing to say to that either.

"Someone is going to lose their job over this," Willis said before he stormed off to his Jeep.

Lindsay had the feeling the someone he was referring to was probably her.

Liam

"That whole two-minute rule thing is bullshit, right?"

Liam looked over at Cross from the passenger seat of the stolen car and then continued to watch the front of the bank before saying, "I wouldn't say that. As far as we are concerned, let's stick to it."

"So, it's real?"

"Well, yeah. I mean, it isn't an exact science—there are too many variables. The cops might get there faster if they're already close by, and they might be slower if some shit happened on the other side of town, but on the average, I'd say it's accurate."

From the back seat, Danny—neither Liam nor his long-time partner Cross knew his last name—pulled his sawed-off Mossberg shotgun with the pistol grip out from under the seat. He said, "Let them come. We'll see how things work out for them."

Liam and Cross looked at each other and then Liam looked back at Danny. "Just be cool. If we do this right, none of that shit is going to be necessary."

"But if it is, are you going to be ready, pretty boy?"

Liam sighed. When a guy by the name of Brownstone came to him with this job, he was aware he'd need a third man. Cross was a reliable driver, but between the guard and customers, Liam couldn't do crowd control and collect the money, especially if he was going to get it all done under the magic two-minute mark.

His normal crowd-control guy had gotten into a fight at a bar, which violated his parole. He would be unavailable for at least the next six months. Mr. Brownstone's intelligence wouldn't last that long, so Liam had acted against his own judgment and brought in Danny on Brownstone's recommendation. Over the last couple of days planning this job, Liam had learned not to like him. It wasn't anything he did or said, but just a general vibe he put out. He seemed too eager to prove he was a tough guy. The fact was, if he did his part, neither Liam nor Cross gave a damn how tough he was.

If Liam put his personal feelings aside, however, it was hardly unusual for a young guy to want to prove himself. Danny seemed to have a high opinion of himself, but he was still a good listener who seemed eager to please. While

Liam liked to trust his instincts, a bad vibe wasn't a viable reason to exclude a guy from his crew. Especially when he didn't have a replacement.

"Don't worry about me," Liam told him. "Worry about yourself."

"I'm not sure. You're putting out a soft vibe right now. This isn't a soft person's kind of gig."

"You ever been to jail, Danny?"

"It's part of the job. Who in this line of work hasn't?"

"Me. Let me tell you why. Because I treat it like a job, and I act like a professional."

"You saying I'm not?"

"Professionals don't get excited about getting in gunfights they can't win."

"You're taking all the fun out of this. I'd heard you were all about the fun. I mean, if you're not having fun, why bother?"

Liam was about to reply when Cross said, "Shut up. The truck is here."

Everyone shut up and watched the armored truck park in front of the bank. If Mr. Brownstone's information was correct, it was dropping off a large amount of cash.

They waited until the truck pulled away and then all three put on old-school hockey masks, the kind the unkillable psychopath from the *Friday the 13th* movies liked to wear, and pulled the hoods of their dark jackets over their heads.

Cross brought the car to a stop right where the armored car had been parked just a few minutes ago, and Danny and Liam exited the vehicle.

This bank liked to have a guard outside, but while the armored car people were doing their thing, he usually got a cup of coffee from the inside break room. Since the armored car people didn't want people standing by the back of the truck while they did the job, he waited inside until they were done. This morning he followed the same pattern.

He was walking out to his post with a cup of coffee in his hand when he saw he was on the wrong end of Danny's shotgun.

"Walk back inside and hit the floor when you get there," Liam told him as he moved past the guard and entered the bank holding his own shotgun.

Liam pointed the shotgun at the other guard who was talking to the bank's lone teller since they didn't have any customers. Thanks to modern technology, people didn't visit the bank like they used to, which also meant the bank didn't have as much cash on hand as they used to—unless it was cash delivery day.

"You can get on the floor on your own or I can put you there," Liam told the guard.

The guard decided to get on the floor on his own.

Liam looked at the teller while Danny shoved the other guard inside. She was a young woman, and she already had her hands up. She looked terrified, which was good. Terrified people usually did what they were told. Despite her look of terror, Liam was sure she'd hit the alarm under her desk. He already had his watch set on the time. He hit the button, and it started counting down from two minutes.

"I'm certain you haven't done anything with the money they just brought, so don't lie to me," Liam said as he pulled the sidearm out of the holster on the second guard's hip and put it in the bag he had slung over his shoulder.

"I wouldn't lie to you..." the teller began.

"Sure you would, but you're not going to today. They brought in two bags. Bring them to me."

"They're heavy..."

"Then bring them one at a time, but be quick about it."

Liam glanced in the mirror to see Danny had disarmed the first guard and put his gun in his bag as well. Once he did that, he moved his gun from one man to the other while sneaking quick glimpses at the door in case someone else came in. Liam hadn't liked the way he was talking in the car, but so far he was doing what Liam needed him to do.

The teller put one bag on the counter and Liam grabbed it and stuffed it into his own bag. He and Danny traded places while she brought the other bag. Liam moved the shotgun from guard to guard while Danny picked up the other bag of cash.

Once he had it, Liam looked at his watch. It read one minute and thirty-seven seconds.

As Danny moved to the door Liam told him, "We've still got like twenty-two seconds."

"So?"

"You wanted to have fun."

Liam figured he would hit the door running but instead, Danny said, "So, we can take our time is what you're saying?"

Liam looked at his watch. "Actually, we used up almost all twenty-three talking about it."

Danny laughed and rushed outside. Liam followed. They both piled into the car. Liam looked back to see the first guard come through the door behind them. He didn't have a gun in his hand, which meant he probably wanted to get the plate number. That would lead to exactly nowhere when the cops ran it.

Danny leaned out his open door and fired his shotgun just before Cross hit the gas. The guard took the blast to the chest and stumbled back inside as Danny pulled himself into the car and they sped away.

"What the hell?" Liam yelled as they hit the road.

"You didn't want him shooting at us, did you?" Danny replied.

"He didn't have his gun."

"You sure?"

"*You* have his gun."

"He could have grabbed his partner's…"

"I have it."

"He must have had a backup."

"He didn't."

Danny shrugged. "I say he did. Either way, he should have stayed down."

"You've made us all murderers."

"Hey, you can't make an omelette unless you break a few eggs."

Lindsay

The FBI did fire someone over the Crumbly incident, but it wasn't Special Agent Lindsay Lane or her partner Smythe. It wasn't Willis either, but he lost his gig in HRT. He wasn't the only one to get transferred. They took both Lindsay and Smythe off the Counterterrorism Division.

Lindsay didn't want a different job within the FBI, and she figured neither did Smythe or Willis. Still, unlike the agent who ordered they start the search of Crumbly's property before it was confirmed Crumbly was in custody, at least they all still had jobs.

When told she could no longer be part of the Counterterrorism Division, Lindsay was asked if she had a preference. She said anywhere but Bank Robbery.

They assigned her to Bank Robbery unit. Smythe asked for Cyber Crimes, figuring the chances he'd ever have to see a teenager get her head blown off were the lowest there. He got his request.

Lindsay never asked Willis if he requested Bank Robbery, but she figured he did because that's what he got. They even got the same field office in Florida. Not that it mattered as much as it used to. Bank robberies had decreased by sixty percent over the last fifteen years; a combination of less cash transactions combined with better security and harsher sentencing was making them a dinosaur when it came to major crimes. The FBI only became involved when the local authorities didn't catch the suspects. Most of the time, would-be bank robbers barely made it out of the bank without getting caught.

Thankfully, she and Willis didn't have to become partners. Since they were both new to the unit, they were each partnered up with a Bank Robbery veteran.

Lindsay was paired with a guy who could have and probably should have retired five years ago named Carson.

Lindsay wasn't eager to report to duty. She'd joined the Bureau to chase down terrorists and for the first five years after she graduated from the academy, she'd done just that. She was good at it too, but she wasn't the only one who joined the Feds hoping to stop the next 9-11 or Oklahoma City bombing. Unlike Bank Robbery, more people wanted to work in Counterterrorism than there were slots available. Lindsay understood there was luck involved in getting a spot and being a qualified female in a profession dominated by men didn't hurt her chances.

While it may have helped get her in the door, she realized it was a detriment when things went south. No matter how many times she proved she belonged in the elite Counterterrorism Division, there was always someone claiming they gave her the job because of her gender.

Lindsay had been given a few days off before she started in Bank Robbery and used those to go visit a prisoner in her home state of Colorado. Going back to Colorado after what happened there didn't appeal to her. If Special Agent Logan was answering her calls, she would have considered joining him wherever the FBI had him, even if it meant as a civilian. Maybe for good.

All that went out the window when he didn't respond to her texts or calls. Her logical mind acknowledged he was maintaining the distance to keep her from knocking his career off track. Their romance could have been trouble for both of them before, but now that she was considered a disgrace, their relationship would be toxic for his career.

Her heart, however, saw it as a betrayal. She couldn't picture herself freezing him out if their roles were reversed.

To make matters worse, she heard from Smythe that he'd had chances to speak up on her behalf but never said a word.

Of course, even if he'd stepped up and stood by her, she'd be making this visit eventually.

She'd been making a point of visiting Sloban Sokolov regularly. The visits had become less frequent once she started working in the Counterterrorism Division, but she hadn't forgotten about him, she couldn't forget about him, and she wanted to make sure he didn't forget about her.

It was a lot easier to walk into the State Penitentiary in Canyon City with an FBI badge than without one. The fact she'd been demoted didn't change what the badge meant to people outside of the Bureau.

Sokolov was sitting behind a thick sheet of plexiglass. She could have had him shackled to an iron ring in an interrogation room instead of seeing him in the standard visitor's area, but Lindsay still had trouble being in the same room with him. The glass was thick enough to not be able to hear the person only a few feet away. An old telephone had to be used.

Lindsay picked up her headset. Sokolov sighed and did the same.

"Hello, Lindsay."

"Call me Agent Lane."

"It's been a while," he told her.

"Did you miss me?" She smirked.

He sighed again. "I'd love to say no, but I don't get many visitors. Among the few I get none but you are an attractive young woman. You look good."

"You don't."

Sokolov smiled, showing off a few gold teeth. The six-and-a-half-foot-tall thug leaned close to the glass before he said, "I can't get my moisturizer in here. I'm sure my skin looks awful."

"I could help with that."

"That would be very kind."

"I wouldn't be doing it out of kindness."

Sokolov leaned back and smiled again. "I admire your determination. How many years have you been coming here to ask me the same question?"

"Answer it and this can be the last time."

"I've already answered it. I answer it every time you ask. Can we talk about something else?"

"We have nothing else to talk about."

Sokolov threw up his hands in mock surrender. "Ask if you must."

"Who hired you?"

"To do what?"

"You know damn well what."

"Do I?"

"Who hired you to kill my parents?"

"I didn't kill your parents."

It was Lindsay's turn to sigh. "Come on, haven't you been in here long enough to drop the act?"

"It appears I have not."

"You were working for Orlov at the time of your arrest."

"Is that a question?"

"Did he order the hit?"

"Orlov was and still is a legitimate businessman. I don't believe he orders hits."

"I think you do believe he orders hits. Otherwise, you would have given him up about a decade ago."

"Given him up for what?"

"For what you're rotting away for."

"Why would Orlov want your parents dead?"

"You tell me."

"I honestly don't know. If someone hires me to do a job, I don't ask why. Even if I did, you think they would have told me why? Such things are irrelevant."

"You'd kill someone without asking why?"

Sokolov shrugged. "The gun doesn't care why you pull the trigger; the knife doesn't care why you're shoving it through someone's heart. I was just an extension of the weapon. Another tool at the disposal of my bosses."

"Which boss used you to kill my parents?"

"Does a gun tell you who pulled its trigger?"

"In your case it did," Lindsay told him, referring to the fingerprints and DNA found on the murder weapon.

"Unlike the gun, I have a choice."

"You're choosing to stay in prison."

Sokolov shrugged.

"Last chance."

"I've already told you everything. Perhaps, if you really want to find out who killed them, you should ask yourself what they did to make someone want them dead?"

"So, I should blame them for being victims?"

"A man who'd hire someone like me wouldn't do so for no reason. It's bad business to kill people for no reason."

"Tell me who hired you and I'll ask them."

Sokolov smiled again. "Aren't you a big-time FBI agent these days? I would assume someone smart like you could figure it out for themselves."

Lindsay was silent for a long time. The fact was, she didn't disagree. She'd yet to find anything to connect her parents to a gangster like Orlov. She'd dug deep into her parents' lives and found some things she wished she hadn't. But there was nothing that would put them in the crosshairs of a notorious Eastern European gangster such as Orlov—or any gangster for that matter. She wasn't about to tell him that though.

Instead, she said, "You'd better hope I don't."

"Why is that?"

"You'll never get out of here unless you help me. You think Orlov or whoever hired you isn't aware I'm a regular visitor?"

"I certainly don't tell anybody."

"Someone does."

"So?"

"So, when I do find them, you think they'll believe I did it without your help?"

"Is that a threat, Agent Lane?"

"Do you feel threatened?"

Sokolov shrugged. "They will believe what they believe. I'll know the truth and that will be enough for me."

"You make yourself sound honorable."

"I sound like who I am."

"You sound like a scumbag piece of shit."

"I can live with that."

"Until you can't."

"Still sounds like a threat."

Lindsay shrugged and hung up the phone.

"Bye, Sloban. I hope to never see you alive again," she said to the glass before she stood. He couldn't hear her, but she had the feeling he understood every word.

They gave her back her phone, purse, and gun at the front of the prison. On her way to the car, Lindsay checked her phone. While she's been wasting her time with Sokolov, she'd received one phone call. It was from a number she didn't recognize, but the area code matched her new field office. The caller didn't leave a voice mail or text. She thought it might be a telemarketing call and the area code might just be a coincidence.

She wanted to ignore the call—if it was a genuine call and important they'd call back—but she changed her mind. If it was her new field office, it would be better to start off making a good impression.

Lindsay returned the call.

"Agent Lane?" a deep voice asked.

"Yes."

"This is Special Agent Cameron Carson, your new partner. Call me Carson, by the way. No one calls me Cameron except my mother."

"Nice to meet you, Carson. You can call me Lindsay."

"I'd prefer Lane."

"Suit yourself. I'm on my way to Florida as we speak. I was under the impression I had a few days before I started."

"You did."

"I don't anymore?"

"I take you're either in Colorado or on your way there?"

"I'm in Colorado now. How'd you know?"

Carson didn't answer her question, saying instead, "I need you to stay there."

"Why, have I been kicked out of Bank Robbery too?"

"Of course not. Quite the opposite. Colorado just had a good old-fashioned bank job and all their people are busy with other stuff, so guess who got the call to come out and assist?"

"You and I?"

"Yep. I'm hopping on a plane as we speak. Meet you at the Denver field office tomorrow morning? They promised us some workspace."

Carson ended the call before Lindsay could offer any opinions.

Liam

Mr. Brownstone owned The Big Bad Bodacious Bar and Grill, a downtown bar that aspired to be a dive. The bar was named after rodeo's most notorious bull and Brownstone leaned into the Western theme as best he could. At one point he had sawdust on the floor and chicken wire around the small stage in the corner. Along with a mounted Brahma bull's head (not Bodacious) over the bar, the neon signs for cheap domestic beer, and some knockoff Western art, the place looked like some backwoods country bar instead of a hole-in-the-wall in the center of a dilapidated mini mall downtown.

Of course, people complained about their shoes getting dusty from the sawdust, so it didn't last. The chicken wire looked cool, but it just made drunks think it was okay to throw bottles at the stage. This led to a huge mess to clean up and seriously pissed off the band, so Brownstone took that down after about two weeks.

He still had the bull, the art, and the neon, though a lot of people looked at the bull mounted like an elk above the bar and asked what kind of asshole hunts cows.

Customers might have thought the western shirt, blue jeans, faux snakeskin boots, and Stetson cowboy hat Brownstone wore was a nod to the theme of his bar, but in fact this is what he wore before he became a bar owner, and if he had his way, would be what he wore long after he was done slinging booze.

Since no one showed up in the afternoon but a few dedicated day drinkers, Brownstone usually worked the bar himself. He was behind the stick cleaning mugs that were already clean when Liam, Cross, and Danny walked in.

Brownstone looked at the duffle bags Cross and Liam were carrying and said, "Meet me in my office."

The trio nodded and headed back through a door at the rear of the bar.

Brownstone looked at his two customers, two daytime regulars nursing tumblers of bottom-shelf whiskey over ice. He considered saying something but didn't. They never messed with him. They'd quietly drink until he got back.

Danny was sitting in Brownstone's chair behind the desk in front of a painting of a man riding a bull that took up almost the entire wall. Liam and Cross leaned against the wall opposite him. The duffle bag was sitting on the desk.

Brownstone shot Danny a look and Danny got out of his chair and walked around to the other side.

Brownstone sat down. He noticed Cross staring at the painting.

"If you're wondering, that is the famous bull Bodacious and the man riding him is me."

"I wasn't," Cross responded.

Brownstone shrugged. He lifted the duffle bag. "Feels a little light."

"Your cut is all there. Feel free to count it," Liam told him.

"My understanding was, we'd do the split together."

"That's what I told them," Danny added.

"You don't trust me?" Liam asked.

"I trust you as much as any other thief."

Liam pointed at Danny. "Your boy was there watching."

"Hey, I'm no one's *boy*," Danny said, turning to look at Liam.

"Shut up, Danny," Brownstone said. "No offense to my *boy*, Danny, but there's a reason I wouldn't hire him to be my accountant."

"There's about a grand more in that bag than you expected," Cross told him.

Brownstone started taking stacks of cash out of the bag.

"The score was more than you hoped," Liam said. "If we wanted to short you, it would have been easy to do, but that's not how I do business. I don't rip off my partners."

After arranging the stacks in a line and seeing there was more money there than he'd expected, Brownstone's expression softened.

"Besides, I thought this could be more than a one-time thing," Liam added.

Brownstone nodded. "For that to happen, we need a level of trust."

"That works both ways."

"I held my end, didn't I?"

"No, you sure as hell didn't."

Brownstone leaned forward. "Excuse me?"

"If we're doing this again, I pick my own crew."

All eyes fell on Danny.

Danny looked back at Liam. "In my opinion, Cross did a fine job driving the car."

"He's talking about you, moron," Cross replied.

Danny stood up. "Who are you calling a moron?"

"Do I really need to explain it to you?"

"Sit down, Danny," Brownstone said.

Cross smiled. "Yeah, Danny sit down."

Danny stayed where he was.

"I will not say it again," Brownstone said.

Danny kept his eyes on Cross. "I don't like being called a moron."

"Then don't act like one," Brownstone said.

Danny sat down.

Once it appeared everyone had calmed down somewhat, Brownstone said to Liam, "I take it you weren't happy with Danny's performance?"

"He killed a man for no good reason," Liam replied. "I don't work with people like that."

"Like what?"

"Like fucking psychopaths."

"He had a gun," Danny protested.

"We've been over that already. You took his gun."

"He had another. He would've had a clean shot at us. I probably saved you a bullet to the back of the head, you ungrateful prick."

"If what Danny says is true..." Brownstone began.

"It's not. There was no gun." Liam snapped.

"You just didn't see it."

Brownstone looked at Cross. "What did you see?"

"I saw nothing either way. I was busy driving."

"So, there might have been a gun?"

Cross shrugged. "It's possible. I trust Liam though. If he says he didn't see a gun, then he didn't see a gun."

"But just because he didn't see it, doesn't mean it wasn't there," Brownstone pointed out.

Cross took a long time before saying, "Yeah, it's possible."

"So, it appears we have a misunderstanding. Gun or not, it appears Danny believed there was one, so he acted. Personally, in what I like to call high-leverage situations, I prefer someone who acts quickly. If you were wrong, there's a good chance you three wouldn't be here discussing the matter."

"I wasn't wrong," Liam said

"It's possible you weren't, but you said you don't work with people who kill for no reason, correct?"

Liam nodded and looked away.

"That would by definition mean you're alright with people who kill for a reason."

"It'd better be a damn good one."

"An armed guard getting ready to unload on you seems a damn good reason to me," Danny said.

"That's not what happened."

"Maybe not, but Danny believed it was happening. Didn't you Danny?"

"Yeah."

"So, if you ask me, your concerns he killed for no reason aren't justified. He may have made a mistake…"

"I didn't..."

"Shut up, Danny. As I was saying, he may have made a mistake, maybe not. Either way, he's not, as Liam put it, a fucking psychopath."

"What does it matter to you who the third is?" Cross asked.

"He's right, fucking psychopath or not, I run the crew," Liam said.

"I feel better with someone I know in the crew," Brownstone stated.

Liam pointed at the money. "You still don't trust me?"

Brownstone shrugged.

"Then I guess our business is done," Liam said as he stood up.

"That would be unfortunate for both of us. I have another job. Same setup."

"Good luck," Liam said as he turned to leave.

"My source of information won't last forever and we only have a couple of days to get ready. I don't have time to find anyone else. Walk away now and we all lose out."

Liam was at the door when Cross said, "Wait."

Liam looked at his partner. "You sure?"

"When have we made that much on a score before?"

Liam couldn't argue with him. He looked back to Brownstone. "Do I have to take Danny?"

"If I said no, could you find a third man in time?"

"Hey..." Danny began.

Brownstone cut him off. "Shut up, Danny."

Liam looked at Cross who shrugged.

"No, we can't."

"Can you two make amends?"

"It's possible I misread the whole thing," Liam said. "I can act like a professional and put this in the rearview if Danny can do the same thing."

"I didn't like being called a moron," Danny said.

Brownstone looked at Cross.

"Sorry," Cross told Danny.

"Good enough?" Brownstone said to Danny.

"Good enough."

Brownstone smiled. "Then let's get to work. We have a bank to rob."

Lindsay

Lindsay stayed in a nice hotel on the Bureau's dime that night and arrived at the Denver field office by nine o'clock in the morning. She wasn't sure what Carson meant by first thing in the morning. She decided for the Bank Robbery unit banker's hours sounded appropriate.

Carson had other ideas. He was already there sitting at his makeshift desk in what had been a conference room. The empty paper coffee cup next to a half-full one told her he either drank coffee quickly or he'd been there awhile.

She stuck out her hand. "Special Agent Lindsay Lane."

He shook her hand, squeezing like he wanted to hear bones break. Lindsay smiled and squeezed back.

Lindsay pointed at an empty desk with a laptop. "That mine?"

"Yeah, but pull up a chair so we can talk."

Lindsay pulled up a chair.

"I like to start at six, seven at the latest."

"Sorry..."

"Don't worry about it. I like to call it a day early too. If you're more of a night person, we can stagger our times. I don't know about you, but sometimes I get more done by myself."

"I feel the same way."

"Good, show up when you want unless I call and ask you to come earlier. That doesn't mean I'm your boss. You can tell me to stay later if you feel the need and I'll do it."

Lindsay nodded. She was getting ready to ask about the case when Carson said, "I can tell, you didn't want to be in this unit."

"I didn't say that..."

"You didn't have to. No one your age chooses to leave an elite, prestigious unit for a dinosaur division like this one. Hell, when I was younger, this *was* the elite unit, and I'd have been pissed if they made me leave."

Lindsay nodded.

"I understand that doesn't make it any better for you right now. I'm saying I get why you might not be happy, but you should be. I assume you know how the FBI started." Carson smiled.

"Someone may have mentioned it back at Quantico."

"Old school gangsters like Dillinger used to get away with taking down a bank just by driving to another state. If it wasn't for bank robbers back in the day crossing state lines, you and I would have had to find a lesser line of work. As far as I'm concerned, the only real FBI agents are in this unit."

"Do people even rob banks anymore?"

"Of course they do. Why do you think you're here in Colorado?"

"I assume it's the First National that got hit a couple of days ago?"

"Yeah, you know why we're here all the way from sunny Florida?"

Lindsay didn't mention she'd never made it to Florida. "They killed a guard?"

"That does make it a priority. Congratulations, you're starting in the big time. Anybody without something better to do is on it."

Lindsay nodded. A big bank robbery paled in comparison to chasing down people looking to bomb federal buildings, but it was clear Carson didn't see it that way.

"I get the feeling you read up on this one."

"Yeah, I figured it wouldn't hurt to read up on any recent robberies and give myself a head start. Though I can't say the media have very much."

"They don't, but there isn't much to tell. Draw any conclusions?"

"Not really. I will say it's been several days. That doesn't bode well."

"No, it doesn't. If we don't nab them within twenty-four hours, we either need to get lucky and have them draw attention to themselves spending the money or get them on the next one."

"Do you expect that they'll spend money foolishly?"

"Most of the time they do."

Lindsay nodded. "I sensed a 'but' in there."

"Yeah, except for shooting the guard, these guys feel like pros. Pros don't go dropping ten grand at the strip club to celebrate robbing a bank."

"So, we wait for them to rob another bank?"

"Not a good option since one of them likes to shoot people. They took the guard's gun and were already driving away. There was no reason to shoot that man."

"So what do we do?"

"Well, I've already been over everything more than once, but you haven't. Read all the witness statements and see if you can spot something that can help us."

"Okay, but these are my first bank robbers..."

"That might be a good thing. Fresh eyes."

Carson stood up. It seemed to take some work. He was carrying more weight around the gut than most agents.

Once he was on his feet he said, "Have fun. Find me when you're done."

"Where are you going?"

"Hit up some informants who won't want to talk if I bring you along. Not that they will have relevant information on anything, but since waiting for the next one isn't an option, I need to do something."

"You have informants in Colorado?"

"Darling, I've been chasing stick-up crews so long I've got informants in places you don't even know are places."

Lindsay nodded and Carson started lumbering toward the door.

Before he left the room, Lindsay called to him, "One question before you go."

"Fire away."

"If they'd assigned you Willis instead of me, would you have called him darling?"

Carson pressed his lips together and smiled. "Probably not. Sorry, I meant no offense."

"None taken. When you run into him you should, though. He likes it."

Carson chuckled. "My keen detective senses tell me that is a load of bullshit."

Carson left the room and Lindsay moved to her own desk. She opened the laptop, found the file on the First

National job, and started reading. There was video footage from the bank's security system, but Lindsay wanted to read the file first before she watched the video.

There really wasn't much to read. Only three people were in the bank and one of them could no longer talk. If he could he likely would have told the same story as the other two. There were other witnesses, people who saw the car parked before it pulled up to the bank, and one person who watched the whole thing from across the street but didn't bother to call anyone.

Not that it would have mattered. The teller hit the alarm, but the robbers were in and out in just under two minutes. The teller mentioned, one robber timed the whole thing. She was on the other side of the room, but she remembered the man who timed everything telling the other man they had twenty-three seconds to spare. She said instead of leaving they waited out the twenty-three seconds.

This was not professional behavior in Lindsay's opinion, but the teller wasn't entirely sure this actually transpired since she couldn't hear them all that well. The guard on the floor by the teller didn't hear any of it, but he said in a statement his hearing wasn't what it used to be.

Lindsay cued up the video to see if they really waited until the two minutes were up.

She watched the video while reading through the teller's statement. Lindsay was glad to see the video backed up how the teller described the event. It meant she was an extremely reliable witness, which in Lindsay's experience was a rare thing.

There was no audio, so she couldn't hear anything, but the two men who entered the bank did pause before leaving. With the faces covered in hockey masks, it was impossible to say if they exchanged words, but from the body language they appeared to have a conversation.

She saw the other guard was close enough to hear it all, but he wasn't talking.

It seemed an important detail to Lindsay. It showed that while the robbers might have been pros to some degree, they were also in it for the adrenaline rush. The two things didn't seem compatible, since a pro would want to minimize risk while someone looking for a rush would want to increase the risk. Unfortunately, she knew someone who this described perfectly.

She dismissed the idea as soon as it popped in her head. However, she pored over the video footage and found a camera angle that captured the two robbers next to the door. Like many businesses, the bank had put what was essentially a ruler next to the exit doors. There were markings every six inches until they reached the top of the door. This enabled any witnesses to get a quick read on a perpetrator's height as they left.

All the witnesses put the robber's height between 5'10" and 6' 2" with one, the second man inside the bank, being shorter than the other but not by a significant amount. Both witnesses said they could not use the door markings to guide them. Neither was looking at the door when the robbers burst in and when they left, the guard was on the floor and the teller behind the counter.

The camera mounted behind the teller, however, was watching the entire time. Lindsay found the angle she wanted and could freeze and then print photos showing both men by the door and the numbers. The witnesses proved to be reliable once more. One man was a shade over six feet tall and the other was a shade under.

Lindsay closely examined the one who was a shade under. The man was her brother's height and the build was right for the last time she saw him. It had been several years, so it was possible her brother could have gained a lot of weight either by working out with weights or letting himself go, and getting fat.

Lindsay had a hard time picturing the latter. He was always into fitness, almost fanatical, but he was never all that interested in pushing heavy weights around that would add to his size. He was more concerned with his ability to scale a wall or run a half marathon than how much weight he could squat or bench.

Of course, being the same size as her brother didn't mean this person was her brother. Sure, if there was a profile on her brother it might match the profile she was developing for the shorter robber, right down to his choice of crimes, but he was far from the only one who fit that profile.

She hoped it was anyone else but him. If the Crumbly incident hadn't ended her career, her brother going back to old bad habits would do the trick.

Carson had yet to return, so Lindsay retrieved her phone from her purse; her personal phone instead of the one the FBI provided for her.

She didn't have to tell her brother why she was calling. All she had to do was get him to provide an alibi without letting him know he was providing an alibi.

He picked up on the second ring.

"Hey, sis, you okay?"

"Yeah, of course."

"You sure?"

"Of course. Why wouldn't I be okay?"

"You called me in the middle of the day and it's not like Christmas or something."

"Sorry, I've been busy."

"I noticed."

"You did?"

"That Crumbly thing was all over the news."

"Who says I was involved in that?"

"More than one enterprising reporter."

"No names were released…"

"You think they don't have their ways?"

Lindsay couldn't argue with him there.

"Hey, I'm not the press. I'm your brother. If you want to talk about it, you can talk to me."

"I'll keep that in mind. I appreciate the offer."

"Anytime. So, what's up?"

"I was just thinking about you is all. Had a few minutes so I picked up the phone and took a chance you'd be available."

"I'm always available for you."

"So, no day job?"

"You mean one where I have to show up at an office or something for a set amount of time?"

"That's kind of the definition of a day job."

"Hell no."

"Still doing that computer thing?"

"You mean building websites? Yeah, as long as I don't have to go to an office and sit there for eight hours. Actually, since Covid companies are more open to hiring people who want to work on their own time. I'm busier than ever."

"Am I keeping you from work?"

"Nah, I don't like to waste sunshine on work."

"I'm with you. Only my job doesn't see things the same way."

"Then you should get a new job."

"The thought has occurred to me. There are days when I wish I was traveling the country in a camper van like you."

"You're always welcome to join me. Tell me where you are, and I'll pick you up."

"Sadly, today is not that day. I take it that means you're still traveling the country in your van?"

"Nah, I'm settling in for the winter. No better place to be for the winter than Colorado. Ski season is just around the corner. I'd make an exception for you though."

"So, you're in Colorado. You got a place in the mountains?"

"Not yet. I'm staying in Denver."

Lindsay wished he would have said he was anywhere else in the world.

"In the van?" she asked.

He laughed. "No, staying at a friend's house."

"Rosa Marie?"

"Who?"

"You two break up?"

"What makes you think we're a couple?"

"I may keep some tabs on my little brother," she told him. She didn't really use the powers of the FBI to watch him, but his name had come up as a known associate for a wheel man named Sterling Cross who was a known associate to a parolee named Rosa Marie Romero. After learning the names of the players, it wasn't hard to figure out Rosa and her brother were more than just known associates of Sterling Cross.

As far as she could tell, Rosa's criminal days were behind her. Having a kid seemed to have cured her of wild ways. Lindsay hoped her brother was following the same path.

"Keeping tabs on me? I'm not sure how I feel about that," he replied.

"I suppose I shouldn't do that and mostly, I don't. Since this cat is already out of the bag, however..."

"We're still friends, but I'm not staying with her. Where are you at these days?"

Lindsay ignored the question. "Is your pal Cross still in the area?"

"Why? You lonely? I suppose I could hook you two up. He always had the hots for you."

"He's not my type."

"You sure? If you're in town, we could all get together."

"I've been assigned to the Florida office."

"Nice. You should learn to surf. We could ride some waves together. How do you like it so far?"

"I haven't got there yet. I'll get back to you on that."

"You mean you'll call me again?"

"Yeah. You know, you don't have to wait for my call. You can call me too."

"I've tried. You're not easy to get a hold of. You've got one of those 'show up at an office for a set amount of time' type of jobs where the set time seems to be twenty-four hours a day."

"Yeah, I suppose you have a point."

"Uncle Corey was asking about you."

"When did you see him?"

"I was in the neighborhood, so I stopped by."

"No one just is in that neighborhood."

"Good rafting and kayaking in the Canyon City area."

"Uncle Corey isn't doing any rafting. He wouldn't be even if he wasn't locked up."

"Yeah, you're right. He's not doing anything but time, but that doesn't mean he doesn't think about you."

"He's not even my real uncle," Lindsay told him. If he had been her real uncle instead of just a friend of her dad's, chances were she might have had a difficult time getting into the FBI since they frown on agents having family members who are professional criminals.

Lindsay was just in the same prison yesterday. It had never occurred to her she might visit her 'uncle' while she was there.

"He still cares about us."

"Does he? Or does he just like the idea of having an in with a federal agent?"

"He's not like that. Sure, he was a thief, but that doesn't make him a bad guy."

"Actually, it totally does. You should stay away from him. He was a bad influence on you."

Lindsay noticed her brother's voice harden. "I thought we weren't bringing that up ever again."

"Sorry, I didn't mean to. Tell Corey I'm fine."

"I will. He's doing good or at least good for a guy in the middle of an eight-year prison sentence, if you're wondering."

Lindsay wasn't wondering but she said, "I'm glad to hear it. When did you see him?"

"I'm not sure, but about two weeks ago? When you don't have a 'show up at an office for a set amount of time' type of job, it's easy to lose track of days."

"A problem I wish I had," Lindsay replied. She was glad to hear he wasn't there yesterday while she was grilling

Sokolov but disappointed it wasn't on the day of the bank robbery. The fact he was in Colorado made it more likely he was in town on the day of the robbery.

"Hey, I made a big deal about my time being my own, but I actually have a work call coming in that I need to take."

"Haven't you told them you don't like to waste sunshine?"

"Oh, I'm going to tell them, don't worry. Promise to call back?"

"Of course."

He ended the call. Lindsay wished she could find out for sure if he was still in Denver on the day of the robbery. She'd make a point of figuring out a way to ask without tipping him before she returned his call.

She'd hoped the phone call would eliminate her brother as a suspect in the First National robbery, but in fact, it had done the opposite. He was in town, and he was still talking to their 'uncle'. He was ultimately responsible for his own actions but there was no doubt Uncle Corey was a bad influence.

Corey loved to tell tales of the outlaw lifestyle and make it sound like a wonderful life. Lindsay guessed he was full of shit from an early age. While for her brother Corey was the coolest dude, Lindsay wondered why her father was friends with the man.

She even asked once. All she got was her mom telling her that Corey and her father went way back.

It didn't help that when Liam ran away from the foster home after their parents died, he'd lived with Uncle Corey.

Lindsay decided she'd give Uncle Corey a visit after all.

Lindsay

She left Carson a message saying she was going to visit an informant of her own and then called the prison to set up the meeting. One perk of being in the FBI was she didn't have to show up on scheduled business hours.

As she made the drive, she pondered over the thing she and Liam had agreed never to talk about again. The promise never to speak of the incident again wasn't the only promise made.

Liam had vowed to leave the outlaw life behind after Lindsay went above and beyond to keep him alive and out of prison. Considering how much she had to lose if the favor she did Liam ever became public knowledge, she really didn't want to believe he'd gone back on his word.

Of course, over the course of her short FBI career, she'd learned more than once that the facts don't care what a person believes. The best way to approach any investigation was to keep an open mind until things were proven or disproven.

She was trying to take this attitude with Liam, but it wasn't easy. Instead of ruminating on her brother's possible betrayal, she turned her mind to the case itself.

The robbers had timed it perfectly. They'd hit the bank just as it received an influx of cash. Before the bank employees had a chance to put it away, they were inside taking the money. They'd literally taken it out in the same bags that cash came in. If the armored truck driver had been looking in his rearview mirror, he likely would have seen them pull up to the front of First National.

These were either the luckiest bank robbers alive or they had someone on the inside.

Yet none of the interviews had pursued this angle.

Lindsay called Carson again. He picked up on the first ring.

Instead of 'Hello' he started with, "I wasn't aware you had local bank robbery informants. You could have told me."

"I didn't either until I was reading the statements and remembered I know an old stick man doing time locally."

"And you think he'd know something about First National?"

"No, not specifically, but it looks like this was the work of professionals and he's the only professional thief I know. I figured he could at least give me some background," Lindsay told him. It was only half a lie. Corey could provide some background on how professional thieves operate, but she was going there to talk about Liam.

Carson didn't need to know that. If things panned out the way she hoped, he never would.

"This professional thief has a name?"

Lindsay didn't want to tell him, but the prison kept records of visitors so he could find out easily enough. "Corey Bronson."

"He robbed banks?"

"No, well, he might have robbed a bank or two, but his thing was more hijacking trucks and stealing from warehouses."

"Organized crime?"

"He was working the fringes and wasn't affiliated with anyone as far as I know."

"I could have hooked you up with a half dozen professional thieves if you just wanted some background. Hell, we have some of them on the payroll."

"Really?"

"Should have asked. How about this, next time instead of telling me after the fact, you run your plan by me first?"

"Like you're my boss?"

"No, like you're my partner. You can do what you want, but since I've been doing this a while, you might find my input valuable. I'd have saved you a drive."

"I think best while I'm driving."

"So, you read the reports and watched the video before heading off to get some background on professional thieves?"

"Of course."

"Any thoughts?"

"Why do you think I called?"

"Tell me."

"The timing is too good not to be an inside job."

"I wondered about the same thing."

"The angle wasn't pursued in the interviews."

"The witnesses..."

"You think the guard and the teller didn't have access to the armored truck schedule?"

"Of course I do. It would be better for them to assume I didn't though."

"Okay, but how about the other people who would know? How come no one has talked to them yet? It's got to be a long list."

"It is. That's why we're spreading it out among the task force."

"What are they waiting for?"

"Not everybody just happened to be in the state."

"You're here."

"Unlike some of our colleagues, I had nothing better to do. If some people had their way, I would still have nothing to do. That's why I got here first. They won't stick me somewhere out of the way if I'm already up and running."

"And they made me your partner?"

"I'd say someone in charge doesn't think highly of either of us."

Lindsay sighed. "So, we've got the busy work while someone else follows the real leads?"

"Welcome to the FBI, Bank Robbery Division Special Agent Lane!"

"I wish I could say I'm surprised. On a more positive note, did your informants have anything?"

"Nope. A complete waste of time."

"I'm almost here."

"I'll talk to you tomorrow then. See you at six?"

"Sure, why not?"

Lindsay used her badge to pull into the parking lot normally used by administrators. It was still surrounded by tall fences topped with rolled razor wire.

The guard who took her stuff recognized her from the day before. "Visiting Sokolov again?"

She shook her head, and he looked down at the ledger. "Corey?"

"You two on a first-name basis?"

"For an inmate, he seems like a decent guy."

"He's not," Lindsay told him as she handed over her gun. Another guard met her at the door and escorted her to the interrogation room. Since visiting hours were almost over, she'd arranged to talk to him here.

The room was plain. There was a table bolted to the floor with an iron ring welded to the middle and two chairs. Corey was sitting in the chair by the wall. He wasn't cuffed to the ring. He'd been a model prisoner and wasn't considered violent.

"I can cuff him if you'd prefer," the guard told her.

"It's fine."

"I can stay."

"We'll be okay."

Corey winked at the guard. "Special Agent Lane and I are practically family."

The guard said, "I'll be right outside."

"Thanks."

Lindsay sat down across the table from her 'uncle.'

"Your brother was here," he said.

"I know."

"He tell you I asked about you?"

"It's why I'm here."

"Finally decided to give your Uncle Corey a visit?"

"You're not my uncle."

"No need to be mean..."

"There's even less need to be nice. Why did you ask about me?"

"Just curious is all. Your dad and I went way back. I realize it was tough on you two, what happened."

"Yes, but the worst part is behind us."

"Sure, but something like that? It never goes away."

"How would you know anything about it?"

"I'm not saying it is anywhere near the same, but your father was my friend, both he and your mom were my friends."

"You're right. It's not anywhere near the same."

"Yeah, I'm right about the other part too, though."

Lindsay couldn't say he was wrong. No matter how busy she stayed or how much time passed, she still thought about them. She didn't tell him that.

Instead, she asked, "How is Liam?"

"You could ask him yourself."

"I'm asking you."

Corey thought about it for a second. "You're worried about him."

"Should I be?"

Corey stroked his beard as he thought some more. "Not that I am aware of. If he's into something, he didn't tell me about it."

Lindsay nodded, then asked, "Okay but when you talked to him, did it feel like he was into something?"

"My feelings aren't admissible in a court of law."

"I'm asking as his sister."

Corey nodded and thought some more before he said, "I honestly have no idea. If I did, I'd tell you."

Lindsay watched him carefully, looking for the signs a person showed when they were lying. Nothing in his tone or mannerisms said he was being untruthful, but the fact was, Corey was an experienced liar.

"Would you?" she asked.

"Yeah, I'd tell Lindsay Lane in a heartbeat if I thought Liam was getting into something bad."

She felt he was telling the truth. The problem was Corey's definition of something bad was probably very different from Lindsay's.

"What about Special Agent Lane?"

Corey shook his head. "I wouldn't tell her jack-shit. You think he's back in the life?"

"No, but it never hurts to check. I prefer prevention over prosecution."

"Well, now that we have that out of the way, how's your life?"

"Could be better."

"Want to tell me about it?"

"No."

Lindsay stood up.

"Leaving so soon?"

"I've got things to do."

"It was nice to see you. We should do this more often."

"Don't count on it," Lindsay said before she turned and left.

She drove back to Denver thinking she'd wasted her time.

Corey

Corey waited while the guard escorted Lindsay out.

The door opened and the guard said, "You know the drill."

Corey nodded but didn't move.

Guard raised his eyebrows. "You're not going to give me trouble, are you?"

"Of course not. I just wanted to talk first. I don't like talking business when I'm in chains and the other person is not."

The guard nodded. "What kind of business?"

"I need to use your phone."

"For what?"

"Just to send a text."

"Okay, the usual fee?"

"Of course."

"Don't solicit a criminal act. I don't want you ordering a hit on a Federal Agent on my phone."

"I am aware of the rules. Besides, I don't order hits."

"Sure you don't," the guard said as he dug his phone out of his pocket and unlocked the screen. Even though the odds of someone coming into the interrogation room were long, he still looked back to make sure no one was watching before he held it out.

Corey reached across the table and took it.

"Be quick about it."

Corey didn't reply as he plugged in the number Liam had given him on his last visit.

He kept it short. "*She knows.*"

Liam

Cross was sitting on the sofa he'd found by the Goodwill box, watching an old movie on an outdated TV, and sipping on a glass of Gentlemen Jack on the rocks when Liam knocked on his door. The room had no other furniture except the couch and a rickety table holding the TV.

"I'm not interrupting anything, am I?" Liam asked as Cross opened the door to his downtown apartment a crack to see who was there.

"If I said yes, would you go away?"

"No."

Cross undid the chain lock and opened the door. He left it open while he walked back to his chair.

"Whiskey?" Cross asked.

"Sounds good."

"You know where to find it," Cross told him as he muted the television.

Cross waited until Liam had poured two fingers of whiskey over ice and sat down in the only other chair in the room before he asked, "Social call?"

"I just wanted to see how you decorated your apartment."

Cross smiled. "Bullshit. You know I hate this place too much to bother making it nice. The city sucks."

"It's only temporary."

"Good thing. Since you're not here to discuss if the sofa matches the carpet, I'm going to guess this is about the job."

"You're like a psychic."

"Let me guess, you think Danny is either an idiot, a psychopath, or some combination of the two."

"I don't so much think it as know it, but that's not why I'm here. My sister called after we left Brownstone's bar."

"The one in the FBI?"

"I only have one sister, so yes, the one in the FBI."

"Okay, how is that a problem? She's in the FBI, but she's still your sister. Sisters call their brothers sometimes."

"Not mine. She seemed to be fishing."

"Like she was investigating you?"

"Yeah."

"Didn't you tell me she was chasing terrorists? You're just a bank robber."

"She was but looks like she's not anymore. She was on a case that didn't go as planned. Some kid died."

"I heard about that."

"The FBI could have moved her. They still chase bank robbers last I checked."

"You could just be paranoid."

"I thought that too, but then my Uncle Corey texted me."

"The one in prison?"

"I only have one Uncle Corey, so yeah, the one in prison."

"Prisoners can text?"

"They can if they pay the right guard," Corey said as he retrieved his phone and pulled up a text from a number he didn't recognize. He showed the screen to Cross.

"She knows. UC," Cross read aloud. "I assume UC is Uncle Corey. Are you sure the 'she' is your sister?"

"Who else would it be? Corey and I don't have a lot of women in common. She must have gone up to Canyon City and asked him about me."

"So, she's here? In Colorado?"

"I think she might be. Which means she lied to me. She said she was in Florida."

"So, she knows something or assumes she does."

Liam drank some whiskey before saying, "Yeah."

"How much do you think she knows?"

"Not too much, or somebody would be sweating me right now in federal lockup."

"You sure? She gave you a pass before."

"She did a lot more than that."

"Exactly."

"Except Danny killed the guard. It would be hard to look the other way even if she wanted to—and I don't think she wants to."

"So she'd bust her own brother?"

"After helping me last time, she was very clear."

"I remember your sister from when we were kids. She didn't seem that mean."

"You only thought she was nice because you wanted to bang her."

"I never said that..."

"You didn't have to. Don't worry, I'm not mad about it. When you have a hot older sister, you need to get used to it, no matter how hard it is."

"Okay, I'll admit it. I had a crush on your sister. Still probably do, to be honest."

"She's a cop. Not just a regular cop but a damn FBI agent."

"That actually makes it hotter."

"I think she has a boyfriend."

"Even better. Makes it more of a challenge."

"Just because I'm used to guys perving on my sister doesn't mean I like it."

"Sorry. What do you want to do?"

"Back out. They could be watching me as we speak."

"So, you brought them here?"

"I took precautions, but it's always possible they're good at this shit and I didn't lose them. It seemed better to do this in person than texting you or talking on the phone. Besides, you're already a known associate. We go back to when we were kids."

"I have a record. If they think you did a bank job, they're going to assume…"

"Yeah, I get it. Better they see me visiting you and drinking your whiskey than having them watch us scouting the Mountain Express Federal Credit Union with Psycho-Danny."

"Yeah, I see your point. So, we're out?"

"Yeah, I don't see another way. I'll figure out a way to get a word to Brownstone without putting any Feds on him."

"If she was already on you, they have Brownstone too."

"She didn't call until after we left, but if they know about him, then they know. No need to make things worse."

Cross nodded. "Money would have been nice."

"Wouldn't have meant shit if we're in custody."

"I suppose you have a point," Cross said, as he dug the burner phone Brownstone had given him for the upcoming job out of his pocket. "No better time than the present."

Cross punched in the number for Brownstone's burner. He let it ring until he got voice mail but didn't leave a message.

"Breaking up by text seems classless," Cross said with a chuckle.

Liam took his phone out of his pocket. "I've never had a lot of class."

"I can't argue with you there."

Liam texted: *We're out.*

"You going to tell him why?"

Liam shook his head. "And you don't either. People like Brownstone knowing I have a sister who's a Fed is a complication I don't need."

"You're right on the money there."

Liam stood up.

"You want to stay and hang out?" Cross asked as he pointed at the TV. "I get like three channels on a clear night."

"Nah, another time."

"You going for a booty call?"

"Hey, if she heard you say that she'd cut off your ear."

"That's why I'm saying it to you and not her. Doesn't make me wrong. Is that where you're going?"

"A gentleman never tells."

"You're no gentleman and that sounds like a yes."

Lindsay

Lindsay had finished a thirty-five-minute run on the treadmill and was completing her workout with the limited selection of dumbbells the hotel workout room provided when her phone buzzed.

When she saw the number on the screen, she almost continued doing curls without answering. After letting it vibrate for a bit more, Lindsay picked it up.

"How's my favorite FBI agent?" Logan said as soon as she picked up.

"You decided it was safe to talk to me now?"

Logan sighed. "Hey, I wanted to talk to you sooner. I wanted to stand by your side."

"But then you might be in trouble too."

"Dating your co-workers, especially if you outrank them, is largely frowned upon—even if neither of the agents involved was part of a highly publicized screw-up."

Lindsay Clenched her jaw. "No one screwed up. Not on my end."

"Hey, just because there were reasons doesn't change what it was. It was a screw-up. A kid died."

"I was there, remember?"

"Agreed. You didn't screw up, okay? I know it but..."

"When things go wrong, someone has to pay." She slumped her shoulders.

"Yeah, sounds like you landed on your feet though."

"Could be worse. I assume you called to break up?"

"Why would you assume that?"

"We work in separate departments now. I'm not even in the same state."

"We could work something out." His voice was a little quieter than usual.

"We hardly saw each other before when we worked out of the same city. This was never destined to work out."

"I travel a lot. There's no reason to think I couldn't end up at the same place you're working for a while."

"So, you want to keep me around as a booty call?"

"I didn't mean it that way."

"Sure, you did."

"Come on."

"When were we not just a hookup?" Lindsay retorted.

"We've been over this, with the job and my divorce..."

"Look, I get it. There were reasons, but that doesn't change what it was."

"It doesn't have to be that way."

"You quitting your job and moving to Florida?" Lindsay asked.

"How about this? You quit yours and stick around Colorado? You're already there. Guess who else is currently working in the Denver area?"

Lindsay didn't reply.

"How about a drink? If you still want to break up with me, wouldn't it be better to do it in person?"

"I suppose you know I'm staying at the Overlook?"

"Of course, that's where we always put up our people."

"Meet you at the bar in about an hour?"

"I could come by your room. Someone in the agency might see us at the bar."

"Bar or nothing. No one is going to think twice about two old colleagues having a drink. Besides, your divorce is final, and I don't work for you anymore."

"Bar it is."

Fifty minutes later, Lindsay walked into the hotel bar and found Logan waiting for her at a high table in the back corner. It really hadn't been that long since she'd seen him last, but she hoped in that short time, he would have deteriorated somehow. In a fair world, his looks would match his personality post the Crumbly Incident.

However, it appeared the opposite was the case. He still looked ten years younger than he actually was, with a face and body that appeared chiseled out of stone. His youthful appearance made it easy for Lindsay to dismiss the dozen years he had on her. She rarely worried her attraction to this particular older man had anything to do with some unresolved daddy issues.

His eyes were still kind and bright blue, always radiating a wisdom that belied his otherwise youthful appearance. The wisdom might have had some truth to it, but she'd known even before he abandoned her, the kindness in those eyes was a lie. Seeing him sitting there in person, however, it was easy to tell herself the opposite.

"I would have ordered for you, but I didn't want the ice to melt," he said as he lifted his own glass of bourbon on the rocks.

"How thoughtful."

Lindsay was going to head to the bar to order but the bartender was already behind her holding a glass of Jack and Ginger ale.

"I assume your drink of choice hasn't changed," Logan said.

Lindsay took the drink and sat down across from him.

He raised his glass. "To the survivors."

Lindsay touched her glass to his and took a good-sized sip before she said, "Is that what we are?"

"You don't think it fits you?"

"It does I suppose. No thanks to you."

"What do you mean by that?"

"You could have stood up for me, kept me in Counterterrorism."

"You have to admit, it could have been worse."

"I suppose it can always be worse. That doesn't mean it couldn't have been better. I've been demoted..."

"No, you've been transferred."

"Feels like a demotion."

"It's not."

"How would you see it if they made you switch to Bank Robbery?"

Logan didn't reply.

"Especially if you did nothing wrong."

"Okay, you're right. I wouldn't like it, but you're not me."

"You saying I deserved this?"

"No..."

"Guess I never belonged in the first place. I was just an affirmative action hire after all."

"I've never said anything remotely like that."

"Just because you never said it, doesn't mean you weren't thinking it."

"Why would I be here talking to you if I thought you didn't belong?"

Lindsay looked him in the eyes. "You're not here for my investigative skills."

"Okay, fair. I'm not. Are you here for mine?"

"I'm not sure why I'm here." She looked away.

"You are here to have a drink with your friend."

"Is that what we are?"

"I'd like to think we are more than that."

Lindsay nodded, but she wasn't sure she felt the same way anymore.

Logan didn't push her for a reply. Instead, he told her, "You shouldn't be so hard on yourself."

Lindsay drank some more before saying, "Actually I'm not hard enough on myself. A kid died on my watch, so probably I'm lucky. Perhaps I deserve much more than a transfer."

"You really believe that?"

"Depends on the day, or more accurately, the minute. I can't unsee it."

Logan nodded.

"I go over everything I did..."

"You were an observer at that point. It was HRT's show."

"Sure, but here's the thing. I can't think of one damn thing we could have done differently."

"They could have delayed hitting his house..."

"Sure, but they weren't there. I'm talking about the people who were there. Sure, the two guys who were supposed to be locals looked more like they were cosplaying rednecks than the genuine article, but Crumbly didn't pick up on that. Willis might be a sexist asshole, but he was right to hold up when the kid appeared and right to move in when Crumbly got the text. Everyone did what they were supposed to do and it all went bad, anyway."

"So, why blame yourself?"

"Because there should have been something we could have done differently."

"Even if Willis was in charge?"

"He was in charge of HRT, but it was my case. If I'd noticed something and told him..."

"You really believe he would have listened to you?"

"Then it would be on him. Instead, it's on me because I missed the fact that Crumbly befriended a kid."

"No way you could have known. All indications are he just met her."

"Speaking of which, any word about who she was? No one returned my calls."

"You're not in the unit anymore."

"I'd still like to know."

"Sorry."

"Are you not telling me because you don't know or..."

"We always keep things close to the vest in Counterterrorism. You should know that as well as anybody." Logan interrupted.

"But I'm not talking to the unit; I'm talking to you."

"I can't."

"Even to me?"

Logan mulled over it for a second before saying, "All I can say is we're still looking for an ID on the girl and we're still monitoring Crumbly's associates. Thanks for that, by the way."

"Thanks for what?"

"All anyone knew you by in the group was a modulated voice."

"So, I made myself easy to replace."

"No, you made it easier to keep on a group of domestic terrorists. We have some of the FBI's best on it and thanks to what you started, we're going to get all these guys."

"So, some of the FBI's best are on it *now*?"

"I didn't mean it that way."

Lindsay took a sip of her drink. "I don't suppose you can give me some details about how you're going to take them down?"

"Listen, I can't. I've probably told you too much already. We need to keep our professional and personal lives separate. Did you ever consider maybe this is for the best?" Logan asked.

"No. Why would I even consider that?"

"It's better for us."

"There's an us?"

Logan noticed the sarcasm in her voice, but he ignored it.

"There should be. Now we don't have to worry about what the department would think. I am no longer a senior officer in your unit. No one can accuse me of using my position to take advantage of you or accuse you of trying to sleep your way into a promotion."

Lindsay felt a flash of anger run through her body. Instead of replying, she took a deep breath and shook her head. Her past experience had taught her it was better to be quiet when the anger inside her tried to surface. Once it was out, she not only worried what she might say but what she might do. Violence was always just around the corner when her temper flared.

Thankfully for everyone, she'd learned a long time ago how to read the signs and regain some measure of control.

Logan wasn't aware of the extent of her potential rage, but he knew her well enough to read the signs that anger was boiling beneath the surface.

He gave a few moments before saying, "I've upset you? Why?"

She finished her drink. "I needed you, Logan. You weren't there."

"Even if I'd begged for you, that you should be kept in the Counterterrorism Division, it wouldn't have done any good."

"Sure, but sometimes it's the thought that counts."

"People already suspected. Hell, your partner Smythe knew, and even though I never admitted it, so did mine. Instead of getting a transfer, you would have been out of a job and so would I."

"That is possible, but put that aside. A kid got killed while I watched and where were you?"

"I had my case..."

"I mean when I needed someone to tell me it wasn't my fault."

"It wasn't your fault."

"Too late."

Lindsay stood up.

"Please sit down. You're right."

"I already knew that. I didn't need you to tell me."

"Please. Let me make it up to you."

Lindsay sat down. "Okay. How?"

"You tell me."

"A kid got her head blown off on my op. I want to know who she was and why she was there."

"Please tell me how talking about the case will help. You need to let it go."

"You asked how you can make it up to me and this is how."

"I can't tell you anything more because that's all the information we have. As far as we can tell she was a runaway who was at the wrong place at the wrong time."

"She have a name?" Lindsay pressed.

"We don't know it yet. Her prints weren't in the system. She hasn't matched any of the missing persons, at least not yet. She was probably eighteen, an adult under the law, so there's no guarantee anyone would report her missing. At some point, someone will miss her and go looking and ideally, we will find each other."

"None of Crumbly's known associates knew her?"

"No one. The best guess is she was hitchhiking and ended up at Crumbly's Stop and Shop. She was probably looking for a ride."

"From the way they talked, it didn't appear that they were strangers."

"It's possible they weren't strangers, but maybe they were. No one actually heard what was being said. They could have just been negotiating a ride."

"He threatened her."

"Negotiations can get heated."

"There has to be more."

"There is, but we don't know it yet. You have same information now about the kid as everyone in your old unit."

"Which is nothing."

"I wish I could tell you more."

Lindsay thought about it for a second and decided she believed him.

He pointed at her empty glass. "You want another?"

"Nah, I'm going to call it a night."

"You sure?"

"It's been a long day. Bank robberies are hard work."

"I've had a long day myself. I could join you."

Lindsay's gut reaction was to say no, but she paused and decided spending the night with Logan beat spending the night alone.

She acted like she was considering it for a minute before she stood up and said, "I still haven't forgiven you but yeah, why not."

Logan smiled. "Are you just going to use me for my body, Agent Lane?"

"Yeah."

"Then I guess I'll pass."

Lindsay shrugged. "Your loss."

She turned and started walking away. She wasn't surprised when Logan said, "Wait, give me a minute to pay the bill."

"Okay, one minute."

She timed him, telling herself if he wasn't ready in a minute, she would leave him at the bar.

He made it in fifty-seven seconds.

Liam

Liam let himself in with his own key.

"That had better be Liam otherwise some motherfucker is going to get a cap in his ass," a voice said from the living room.

Liam peeked around the corner. "Don't shoot."

Rosa raised her empty hands. Liam took a moment to take her petite body in before he walked over and sat by her on the couch. As always, he was blown away that a woman who looked like her was willing to put up with a guy like him.

"You're late," she told him as she scooted away.

"Sorry."

"Ian wanted to see you."

"Well, I'm here. Where is he?" Liam replied. He was here to see Rosa, but he liked her kid. He didn't see himself as parenting material, but the kid seemed to like him too.

"Ian is five years old. He has a bedtime."

"That's no fun."

"Didn't you have a bedtime?"

Liam shrugged. For much of childhood, he didn't. When he ran away from foster care and got taken in by his criminal 'uncle' bedtimes became a thing of the past. He didn't say that to her. The fact was he would have traded anything to have his parents still be alive and send him to bed when the clock hit a certain hour.

Instead, he said, "You really think he's asleep?"

"No, he's probably playing games on his tablet under the covers, but that's not the point. Where were you?"

"I had some business."

She almost asked what kind of business but then she shook her head. "Don't tell me about it, okay?"

"I wasn't planning to."

"Good, I like this better when I can pretend you're not an idiot."

"An idiot?"

"All the outlaws I've ever known have ended up dead or in prison."

"You're neither of those."

"Because I left the outlaw life behind me. I'm an exception. Since this is always the way things end up..."

"I can be an exception too."

"They all say that. Every last one of them."

"You said that."

"Yeah, doesn't change the facts."

Liam scooted close to her. "I'm still alive and free right now."

"Good for you."

"How about you take advantage of that fact before..."

Rosa leaned over and kissed him. He kissed her back.

When the long kiss ended she said, "You want to play some games under the covers?"

"You don't have to ask me twice."

Lindsay

Lindsay woke up before Logan. She was showered, dressed, and ready to go before he stirred.

He looked and saw her heading for the door and asked, "Is the sun even up?"

"My new partner likes to start early."

"That's because he's old. Bedtime is probably dusk."

"You're not wrong. Don't be here when I get back."

"See you tonight then?"

Lindsay wanted to say no, but went with, "We'll see."

She left the room and saw Willis in the hall.

"They send you here too?" he asked.

"I wouldn't be here if they didn't," she said as she passed the elevator and headed for the stairs.

"Too good to share an elevator with me?"

"I get it, your ego has difficulty with this concept, but not everything is about you. In fact, when it comes to me, nothing is about you."

"You just like the exercise?"

Lindsay shrugged.

"Makes sense," Willis said as he followed her to the door, "I like exercise too."

"You going to take the stairs with me?"

"I was going to take stairs, and you just happened to be there. It's not all about you."

Lindsay ignored that and headed down the stairs. Willis followed.

"I wanted to tell you something," he said as he caught up to her.

"Yeah?"

"I didn't blame you for the Crumbly thing."

"Seemed like you were blaming me at the time."

"I was upset. When I could objectively scrutinize it again, I saw it differently. My report and the debriefing reflected that."

"For the record, I didn't blame you either. Yet here we both are."

"Yeah, well, a kid still died."

"Yeah, I suppose there's no getting around that. Are you working the First National case or did another bank get robbed?"

"First National. The bigger question is why Special Agent Logan is in town? I saw him at the bar last night drinking alone."

Lindsay suppressed a laugh. "Hard to say."

"He took over Crumbly."

This was news to Lindsay. He never said he was working on the Crumbly case. "What was there to take over?"

"Apparently Crumbly had some connections. The intel says that whatever big thing he was planning wasn't going to be a solo endeavor."

"Please stop. I'm not sure I want to know."

Willis shrugged. "You don't miss it?"

"Of course I miss it. That's why I don't want to hear about it. Do you miss HRT?"

"No, not even a little bit."

"You're glad they moved you?"

"I asked them to."

"Why?"

"Do you have to ask?"

The image of the dead girl sliding out of Crumbly's grip as she left a trail of blood and brains on his shirt flashed into Lindsay's mind. She realized Willis was right. There was no need to ask.

Liam

Liam was walking out of Rosa Marie's apartment building when he saw a familiar car parked in the lot. He stopped and looked closely and saw it was not only the vehicle he'd seen Danny arrive in when they met at Brownstone's bar but Danny himself was sitting in the driver's seat looking at his phone.

Liam didn't think Danny had seen him, so he went back inside the building and used the exit on the other side. He worked his way around the parking lot and approached the passenger side. He tried the door and found it unlocked.

Danny looked over when the door opened. He reached for something under the seat but stopped when he saw it was Liam.

Liam sat down next to him.

"You scared me," Danny said with a laugh.

"What are you doing here?"

"Waiting for you."

"Why would you wait for me here?"

"This is where your girl lives."

Liam didn't like Danny knowing about Rosa Marie. He was certain he'd never mentioned her and knew he'd never said where she lived.

"What makes you think that?" he asked. He wished he'd gone by his car first and grabbed his gun. He had a feeling this might turn ugly.

Danny shrugged. "Brownstone told me. I mean, you're here, so there must be something to it."

"I like to keep my personal life and my work separate."

"Okay, I didn't mean nothing by it. He didn't tell me her name or anything. Just the building."

Liam was glad to hear that, but his relief wore off when he realized just because Brownstone didn't tell Danny her name and apartment number, it didn't mean he didn't know.

"Keep it that way," Liam said as he opened the door.

"Wait, Mr. Brownstone wants to talk to you."

"I've got nothing to say to him right now. I'll call him when I do."

"Look, I know what you're saying, but he will not accept it. You might as well just talk to him."

"Why?"

"He wants to find out why you and Cross backed out. Possibly it's something he can help you with."

"Unlikely."

"Sure, but he thinks you owe him an explanation. I don't think he's wrong."

Liam considered it briefly. If someone he was planning a job with sent a two-word text, he might want an explanation too.

"I suppose I owe him that much. I'll meet him at his bar in a couple of hours like before."

"Why don't we just go over now? You're already in the car."

"I'll meet him in his bar in a couple of hours or I won't meet him at all."

"Okay, I was just trying to make things easier. See you in a couple of hours."

Liam wanted to ask why Danny needed to be there but decided it didn't matter. He opened the door and got out without saying another word.

Lindsay

Lindsay beat Willis to the makeshift office although they left at the same time. She'd texted Agent Carson once she got in the car, asking if he wanted her to stop and pick him up a coffee on her way to the office. He told her he'd already picked up a cup for both of them. Willis's partner wasn't so thoughtful so he had to make a stop on the way.

Lindsay took her coffee from Carson. "How'd you know I'd be coming in early?"

"Just a hunch."

Lindsay took a sip. "How'd you know how I like it?"

Carson shrugged. "Another hunch."

"You're two for two. Any other hunches? How about a line on our bank robbers?"

"I'm not doing as well on that as I am on coffee orders. We've got the employee list from Brunson Logistics and Security."

"The armored car company?"

Carson nodded and pointed to the well-dressed man sitting on the other side of the room. The man didn't bother to look up from his computer. "That's Special Agent Emilio Gomez, he'll be working with us along with Agent…"

"Willis. We've met."

Carson nodded as he realized where they probably met. "Willis and Gomez have the bank employees and family members. We have the armored car people. The inside tip pretty much had to come from one or the other."

"So, we're all staring at our computers today."

"We can't visit the prison every day. That would be too much fun."

"You want the first half of the alphabet or the second?" Lindsay asked Carson as Willis came through the door carrying two coffees.

He nodded at Lindsay and Carson and then held out a cup to Gomez. Gomez took the cup without looking up. He motioned with his head to Willis's desk and Willis sat down and started reading up on the employees at First National.

"I already started on the names beginning with A," Carson said, "so why don't you start in the Ms?"

Lindsay nodded. "I'm new to this. I can spot the red flags for terrorists; not sure what to look for to identify a bank robber."

"Narrow the list down to people who would have known cash delivery times first. Don't leave out people who shouldn't know but have access to those that do. A janitor or receptionist wouldn't have access to that information, but if they ran across someone who did..."

"People talk."

"Yeah, just as often it's someone like that as it is a disgruntled manager. We cast a wide net and then do a deep dive into everything the internet knows about whoever we catch."

"Sounds time-consuming."

"It is, which is why we should get started. It's why the normally chatty Agent Gomez is being so anti-social. Hell, they don't even have half as many names to go over as we do."

Gomez showed Carson his middle finger without looking up from his computer.

Lindsay made her way to her desk. She saw Carson had already emailed her the list of employees, starting from those with last names beginning with M.

She started reading.

Liam

Liam parked behind Brownstone's bar. He took his Glock 19 out of the glove compartment and dropped the magazine. Inside was a full mag, fifteen rounds in all. He slapped it back in and put it in the small holster in the small of his back.

"You think that will be necessary?" Cross asked.

"Better to have it and not need it than the other way around. Speaking of which..."

Liam reached under the seat and produced an S&W Police Special 0.38 already in a holster with a Velcro strap. He opened the cylinder and saw five slugs. The slot for the sixth sat empty under the hammer.

"You're missing a bullet," Cross told him.

"Makes it harder to shoot your dick off this way," Liam said as he strapped the holster to his ankle and pulled his jeans over it.

"You'd have to be one unlucky motherfucker to shoot your dick off with a gun strapped to your ankle."

"Yeah, even if I'm not that unlucky, I'd hate to find out the hard way my luck is worse than I anticipated. Besides, I've got twenty rounds on me between the two guns. If I need more than that, probably it'd be a losing cause anyway. You carrying?"

"Should I be?"

"I don't know. Having Danny show up outside Rosa's place rubbed me the wrong way."

"Like he was telling you something?"

"Exactly! And it wasn't something good."

"I felt the same way when you told me about it," Cross said as he turned his hand to reveal a silver Raven MP-25 with faux walnut handles. The small gun fitted nicely into Cross's larger-than-average hands.

"A Saturday Night Special?"

"It's new and improved. Plus, I can palm it."

"Not a lot of firepower. If shit goes down, will it be enough?"

"Hard to say. You could stand against the wall over there and we could test it out."

"No thanks."

"I'm guessing anyone else I point this at will feel the same way."

The two men got out of the car and walked around the building to the front. They didn't want Brownstone to be aware they'd parked in the back.

They figured this time of day he'd be behind the bar, but instead of Brownstone, there was a young blonde woman wearing cut-off shorts, a halter top that looked two sizes too small, and a black cowboy hat.

They took in the rest of the bar. Two regular day drinkers were sitting in the same spots they were the other day. The only other customers were a large man, both in height and girth, and a guy who might be five feet tall if he stood on his toes. They were splitting a pitcher of cheap beer at a high table in the back of the room. In the low light, it was hard to tell too much about them other than their sizes. Liam didn't suppose the FBI or even the local cops let their people get that fat or took many guys that short, so it was unlikely they were the law staking out Brownstone.

The woman behind the bar smiled. "I bet you two boys are here to see the boss."

Cross smiled back. "You'd win that bet."

"He's in his office waiting for you two. Tiny and Big Jim will show you the way."

From the table, the two men emerged. The big one was bigger than Liam thought with a long beard that appeared to have been grown to make up for the total lack of hair on top of his head. His sleeves were rolled up, showing off a lot of tattoos that had the prison ink look. They saw at least one swastika on his inner forearm right next to a circle containing two arrows and a skull.

"You Liam?" he asked.

"I take it you're Big Jim?"

"Nah, they call me Tiny. This here is Big Jim."

The short man came around his big friend so they could get a better look at him. He was almost a miniature version of Tiny only with less fat and more muscle. His beard wasn't quite as long, but his head was just as bald. Unlike Tiny he'd added a few tattoos to his clean dome, including a matching two arrows and a skull tattoo by his right ear.

"Those names ironic?" Cross asked.

Big Jim grabbed his crotch. "Not mine for sure."

"Mr. Brownstone wanted us to check if you two were armed," Tiny said.

Cross lifted his shirt without letting them see the Saturday Night Special in his palm and spun around. "Not me boys."

They nodded and looked at Liam.

Liam took the Glock out of the holster from behind his back and held it up without putting his finger on the trigger and said, "The answer is yes," before putting it back behind his back.

"Mr. Brownstone would like you to leave it behind the bar with Misty. You can have it back after you're done."

"And if I say no?"

"It won't work out well for you," Tiny told him.

Liam noticed Big Jim moving his hand behind his back.

"Tell your little buddy to keep his hands where I see them or it won't work out well for you either."

"Don't call me his 'little buddy'."

"Hey, Liam, just leave the gun. We didn't come here for trouble," Cross said.

"Yeah, Liam, leave the gun," Big Jim said as he kept his hand behind his back.

"Damn Jim," Tiny said, "no need to be escalating this shit. Put your hands back where they can see them."

"I don't like being called 'little buddy'."

"That reason enough to go all high noon in Mr. Brownstone's place of business?"

Big Jim didn't have an answer.

Tiny looked at Liam. "Same goes for you. Is hanging onto that shooting iron worth getting into a gunfight over?"

Liam shrugged and unclipped the holster. He turned to Misty behind the bar.

"Don't worry, cowboy," she told him, "I can handle your pistol."

"She's something of a pistol-handling expert," Big Jim said.

Misty gave him a dirty look.

"You can handle my big pistol anytime, darling," Big Jim added.

Misty looked like she had something to say but kept it to herself. She held out her hand and Liam placed the gun in her palm. She put it under the bar and said, "Don't worry, cowboy, it will be waiting for you."

"I'm no cowboy."

"Sure you are. You wouldn't be here if you weren't."

"Follow us," Tiny said.

"No need, we've been there before," Liam told him.

They moved out of the way and Liam and Cross made their way to Brownstone's office. Neither Tiny nor Big Jim followed.

"I don't like this," Cross whispered before Liam opened the door.

Liam nodded and they entered the room.

Brownstone was behind his desk looking at his laptop. In the corner, Danny was leaning against the wall looking annoyed.

"Well," Liam said, "I'm here to tell you in person…"

"Have a seat," Brownstone said.

"No need. I'm out and so is Cross."

"Why?" Danny asked.

Liam turned his gaze toward Danny. "I suppose that is a fair question. I got word a Fed has a hunch I was involved with the First National job."

"Word from who?" Brownstone asked.

"A reliable source. Doesn't matter to you. What matters is they may be watching me and since they know Cross and I are known associates, they might be watching him too. If we go through with this, there's a good chance we all go to jail."

"Bank robbery is a risky business," Danny said. "I figured you were all about the adrenaline anyway? Higher risks equal bigger thrills."

"There's taking risks and then there's being a dumbass. This falls under being a dumbass."

Brownstone motioned to the chairs in front of his desk. "Sit down, please."

"I don't see why I need to bother," Liam told him. "I've got nothing else to say."

"Well, I do," Brownstone replied, "and I prefer to say it while you're sitting down."

Liam sighed and looked at Cross. Cross shrugged and they both sat down.

"Thank you," Brownstone said.

"Say what you're going to say. I've got things to do."

Brownstone smiled. "What if I told you I had sources in the FBI too?"

"I'd tell you I don't care."

"My source says we're clean. Sure, your name may have come up but no one is looking at you yet."

"I need more than your word before I stick out my neck."

"Alright."

Brownstone turned the laptop around so they both could see it.

A video began to play. As the video started, Tiny and Big Jim entered the office and stood behind Liam and Cross. They both turned around.

"Don't worry about them," Brownstone said. "Worry about what's on the screen."

Liam turned toward the laptop. He took note he could see both men's reflections in the glass covering the huge bull riding painting behind Brownstone's desk. He kept one eye on them as he turned the rest of his attention back to Brownstone's laptop. Liam reached down as if he was scratching his lower leg and lifted his pant leg up so it was out of the way of his gun.

Liam right away recognized the parking lot the unseen cameraman was filming. He and Cross watched Rosa Marie emerge from her apartment with her son holding her hand.

"Nice piece of ass you got there," Big Jim said.

Brownstone glanced at him sharply and Big Jim shut his mouth.

The camera stayed on her as she got to her car and strapped Ian into his car seat.

"What the hell…?" Liam began.

"Wait, the good part is coming up."

The camera followed her car as she drove away and then the screen went blank for a second before coming back inside her apartment. The camera moved through, taking in both her and Ian's bedroom before going blank again.

"Why are you filming my friend's apartment?" Liam asked.

"Just wanted to show you how easy it would be to get to her."

"You threatening her?"

"No, not yet. It doesn't have to come to that."

"You'd better hope it doesn't."

Brownstone shrugged as he turned the laptop back around. He looked at Cross. "Do you want to see some video of your cousin and her kids? I hear she's one of the few family members who visited you during your time as a guest of the state."

"This is a bad idea on your part."

"All I need is for you two to finish what we started. If I thought we were compromised in some way, I would be fine calling it off, but we're not. My source for the armored car routes will dry up sooner rather than later. This is probably the last job for a while anyway. Finish it, and we can all walk away happy."

"If we don't?"

"I might give that nice little piece of ass a visit," Big Jim said with a laugh.

"Say it again," Liam said without turning around.

"Why? You didn't hear me the first time?"

"I like to be absolutely sure I heard what I thought I did before I kill you."

Liam looked at the painting behind Brownstone. In the reflection of the glass protecting the painting, he could see Big Jim tense up. Liam let his right hand hang down so he could reach the gun.

"Come on now," Brownstone said, and Big Jim seemed to relax a little. "There's no reason for any hostility. No one is watching us. There is no reason not to do the job. This way, we all get paid and after that, you can walk away on good terms."

"I don't like being forced into things," Liam told him.

"I understand. If I had more time to find someone else, I would gladly let you go on your way, but I don't."

"Why is this so important to you?" Cross asked.

"It's what people in your line of work call a big score."

"There will be other big scores."

Brownstone nodded. "I need the money now. I have obligations to people who wouldn't take kindly to me not living up to them."

"What obligations?" Liam asked.

"That is my business. Needless to say, they have put me in a position where I have to take extreme measures. We can, of course, avoid all of that just by you two doing what you're good at."

Cross looked at Liam. "Come on, Liam, we can do this one. We can go dark until the day of the job in case someone is watching?"

Liam seemed to be lost in deep contemplation.

"Winter's just around the corner," Brownstone said.

"Yeah, so?" Liam said half distracted.

"So, you both are going to want to spend it on the slopes. You think I don't know you both do crime to fund your ski-bum lifestyle?"

"You know a lot, but that doesn't mean you own us," Liam told him.

"There is one thing I don't know. Your last name isn't Kilmiester, Liam."

"It is as far as you are concerned."

"Come on, we're friends here. What is it?"

"Go to hell."

"Interesting name. It must have been awkward when they called roll at school."

"Are we done here?" Liam asked.

"I'm still waiting, I haven't gotten an answer."

Liam looked at Cross.

Cross shrugged. "If we pull it off right under the Fed's noses, how cool would that be?"

Liam paused for a long second before saying, "Alright, your source says we're cool, then I'm going to trust you."

"I haven't steered you wrong yet."

"We're going into hiding until the day of the job. Don't contact us."

"As long as you remember to show up."

"I wouldn't miss it for the world," Liam said as he pushed his jeans back over the gun on his ankle.

They both stood.

"You still want to kill me, tough guy?" Big Jim asked.

"If I did, you wouldn't be around to ask dumb questions," Liam told him. "Now get out of my way, little buddy."

Big Jim gave Liam a hard glance. Liam held his gaze. Tiny tapped Big Jim on the shoulder, and Big Jim moved out of the way.

"You shouldn't antagonize him," Tiny said as they walked by.

Liam ignored him and walked out of the office. The pair of tattooed thugs followed them into the bar and returned to their pitcher of beer. Liam stopped at the bar.

"You want a drink?" Misty asked.

"Just my gun."

"Not a drinker?"

"No, I like a drink now and then. I'm just particular about my company."

She smiled as she reached under the bar. When she bent over, Liam got a good view of her cleavage. He was sure this was intentional.

She stood up with his gun in her hand. "I imagine you'd find me mighty fine company if you gave me the chance, cowboy."

Liam took his gun. "Possibly I would, but not today."

He put the gun behind his back before he and Cross left.

Back in the car as they were driving away, Cross asked, "Do you really want to do this? We could scoop up Rosa and Ian and take them to the cabin and then figure out how to handle Brownstone and his crew."

"She wouldn't like that."

"No, but she's a realist. She'd be pissed but she'd understand."

"What about your cousin and her family?"

"They're not as practical. I don't see them going to the cabin with us."

"You're not worried?"

"The best he could do was threaten my cousin who lives in Nevada? He was blowing smoke on that one."

"But not on Rosa Marie?"

"It didn't feel that way to me. She's local, and let's be honest, I'm always going to follow your lead. Even when I shouldn't."

Liam nodded. "There's something wrong with all of this. Suddenly Brownstone has some Aryan Nation-looking thugs watching his back? He didn't shoot that video yesterday and until last night he had no reason to want to hold her safety over my head. This is more than some struggling bar owner looking to make some extra cash."

"I agree. Is that a reason not to do it?"

"No, the easiest way out of this mess might still be to just do the job, get our money, and get ready for winter."

"The money would be nice."

"Can't argue there."

"So, we do the tail shake and head to the cabin?"

"Yep."

Cross headed toward the parking garage where they kept the spare car.

Mr. Brownstone

Danny sat down in the chair previously occupied by Liam.

"You got something to say?" Brownstone asked him as he messed with his laptop.

"Why do we need them? We got Tiny and Big Jim here now, plus the twins and Misty. Hell, I can find a bunch of guys who could drive a car..."

"None of those people are bank robbers."

"You say that like it is brain surgery."

Brownstone moved his laptop to the side and leaned forward so he was looking Danny in the eye. "I don't have to explain myself to you."

"I get it, but it wouldn't hurt morale none if everyone understood why we're going through so much trouble to keep these two around when we don't need them."

"You get the sense morale is down?"

Danny shrugged. "I'm just saying questions might get asked."

"You're not part of the planning phase, Danny. There's a reason for that."

"No need to be mean."

Brownstone leaned back. "I'm just being honest. You really think if you, Tiny, and Big Jim hit the First National it would have gone so well?"

"Maybe, maybe not, but it doesn't matter. I've seen how it's done now."

Brownstone shook his head. "Perhaps next time. I just want you to have a little more experience before you lead the fundraising crew."

"Really? I'd lead the crew?"

"No, of course not."

Danny hung his head.

"You do your job well, Danny. I'm not kidding when I say this. Don't screw us all up trying to do jobs you're not good at."

"I guess…"

"Don't guess. I take it from your tone you don't like our bank-robbing partners."

Danny shrugged. "They're okay."

"Well, don't get too attached. After this job, they're going to be a liability."

Danny nodded. "You just tell me when."

"I'll do that, Danny. Have Misty bring me a bourbon, would you?"

"Sure," Danny said as he stood. He may not be able to plan a robbery, but he understood when he was being dismissed.

It wasn't long after Danny was gone and Misty brought the bourbon there was a knock on Brownstone's door.

He was about to tell Danny to go away when the door opened and two men walked in.

"You probably shouldn't be here," Brownstone told the men known as Blondie and Blackie. The Corsica brothers were twins, identical except for the color of their hair, though those colors weren't the ones they were born with. One dyed his hair jet black and the other chose bleach blond.

"We made sure your patsy was gone," Blondie said.

"What do you want?"

"I'm worried about our role in your little plot," Blackie said.

"How so?"

"You seem to have us on the sidelines for the dirty work. Considering our skills, do you think that's wise?"

"You two know you're the smartest most reliable people we have right now?"

"We do, which is why we're asking why you're trusting Big Jim and Tiny..."

"You'd rather I trust them with the money?" Brownstone interrupted.

Neither twin had a good answer for that.

"Don't worry, when this is over, someone's still got to take care of Danny," Brownstone added. "He's a good kid, for a moron and psychopath, but he's not down with the cause."

"You ask him?"

"We already have enough morons and psychopaths in our ranks."

This seemed to satisfy the twins.

"Get out of here," Brownstone told them. "We don't need to be seen together."

The twins left.

Lindsay

"How's it going?"

Lindsay leaned back and looked up at Carson. "Slow."

She wasn't kidding. She was going through the drivers and the crew members who had access to the schedule. It seemed as if it should be a limited number, but Brunson Logistics had six trucks and each truck would carry a crew of at least three. To keep things going all week, they had twenty-four drivers or crew members working full time and another six who worked part time. While each crew should be only responsible for their own pickups and deliveries, Brunson's management admitted all the drivers had access to the entire schedule.

These thirty men were all carefully vetted, with a lot of ex-cops and ex-military in the mix. No one had anything on their record that would jump out as a red flag. This meant Lindsay had to expand her search into just about anyone they would come in contact with, starting with family members.

Unfortunately, Lindsay knew all too well being a good citizen didn't mean your loved ones weren't operating on the wrong side of the law.

Carson nodded. "Slow, that's usually how it goes around here until it doesn't."

"Yeah, it wasn't too much different in Counterterrorism."

Willis looked up from his computer. "Same with HRT, only with less reading."

"So, worse?" Lindsay asked.

"No, better. We trained. This makes me miss five-mile runs in full gear."

Everyone looked at Gomez to see if he had anything to add to the conversation. He never looked up from his laptop.

"I had an idea that might speed this up, though," Lindsay said.

"I'm listening," Carson replied.

"Can we get the cash drop-off schedule?"

"Why?"

"Just curious when and where the next big drop-off is."

"You figured you'd do like our crew and make some cash?"

"No. You can tell me if I'm wrong since I'm new at this, but it seems to be from what I understand, robbing a bank isn't usually a one-time thing, assuming they get away with it the first time."

"I'd say that's accurate. Actually applies to the amateur more than the pro since for the amateur it isn't all about money. This group falls more into the pro category, in my opinion."

"Sure, but they did wait until the two minutes were almost up and one of them killed a man for no discernible reason."

"So, you think they're a mix of the two?"

"You're the expert, not me, but yeah. I would think these guys aren't that different from people who get involved in terrorist organizations. Some are just bored and looking for thrills. They like running around playing army in the woods getting ready for the big race war they know will never happen. For others, there is no element of thrill-seeking; they're in it because they really believe. They're running around with their guns in the woods and learning to make bombs because it is their strong belief they're going to need those skills to survive. Most people, however, fall somewhere in the middle."

"They might really believe, but they also really enjoy running around the woods with assault rifles?"

"Exactly."

Carson considered that for a moment. "I suppose it's the same, only it's about money instead of ideology. I would say professionals don't like to work with amateurs."

"If they don't like it," Lindsay pointed out, "that would say they still do it once in a while."

"Sure, there's not all that many actual professional thieves."

"So, in your expert opinion, what are the odds they're going to try it again?"

"If I were a betting man, I'd put my money on yes."

"If they have someone on the inside giving them intel, what are the odds they only gave them First National?"

"Low. The inside man might get an adrenaline rush over screwing over his company, especially if he's disgruntled, which they usually are, but for him or her it's not really about the thrill. It's a combination of money and revenge. One time is often enough, plus if they have a shred of common sense, they should be aware every time they give up something the odds of getting caught grow exponentially. Especially if they know we're looking at them."

"Do they know?"

Carson deliberated for a moment. "Depends on what level of employee was passing information. Most shouldn't be aware their company gave us their employee list. We advised against telling the employees we were looking at them. Of course, if they have half a brain, they'd have known we were going to."

"If they had half a brain, they wouldn't have passed the information in the first place," Willis added. "We shouldn't assume they're stupid, but it's just as bad to assume they're smart. Like you Agent Carson, I'm not a bank robbery expert, but if they're like most criminals, they tend to fall on the dumb side."

"You're not wrong, Agent Willis," Carson said. He looked back at Lindsay. "So, you're thinking we might be able to spot their next target?"

"Yeah. Seems worth a shot."

"Waste of time," Gomez said without looking up.

"Why's that?" Lindsay asked.

"You want us to put resources into staking out a bank they might hit? What if they don't show up?" Gomez asked.

"What if they do?" Willis asked.

"They won't," Gomez said. He looked up from his computer and focused on Carson. "You should know better, old-timer."

"I'm not sure I do," Carson replied.

"You should. We catch them with patience and research. The inside man is on here somewhere. We find them and they give up the rest."

"Why not a little of both?" Lindsay asked. "The files will still be here waiting for us either way."

"As I said before, waste of time."

Carson opened his mouth to say something but Gomez held up his hand. "I'm the agent in charge and I say it's a waste of time. The only bigger waste of time would be to sit here arguing about it."

"Of course," Carson replied, "I wasn't going to argue. I was going to tell you Lindsay and I are going to get some lunch. We might be a little late coming back."

"Then you're going to stay late to make up for lost time."

"Of course."

Liam

Cross pulled the car into the garage and found a spot to park. The two of them spent a few minutes to scope the area to see if anyone might be watching. When it appeared the coast was clear, Liam dug a quarter out of his pocket.

"Call it," he said as he flipped it in the air and caught it in his palm then covered it with his other hand.

"Heads."

Liam lifted his hand and the bust of George Washington was showing. "Two out of three?"

"Nope."

They left Cross's souped-up Toyota Corolla and made their way to the old Jeep they kept parked on the bottom floor of a downtown parking garage. Liam climbed into the trunk and put the blanket they kept there over him.

Cross found the cowboy hat, glasses, and jean jacket in the front seat. He put all three on and tucked his hair under the hat. Though it wasn't much of a disguise, it would be enough for anyone watching the garage to see him driving a different car without Liam and assume it wasn't him. If someone really was watching them, they'd figure out fairly quickly, but by then he and Liam should be well away.

Cross kept the speed a touch over the legal limit as they made their way out of town, heading west on I-70. He kept his eye on the rearview mirror and took a detour through Idaho Springs that made no sense, which was the idea. The only reason for anyone to match his route would be if they were following them.

No one matched the route. They stopped for gas in the next town and Liam climbed out of the trunk.

"Enjoying the ride?" Cross asked.

"Next time we aren't flipping a coin. You get the trunk."

"But I'm the better driver."

"It's driving. They let teenagers do it."

"I'm still better."

"Don't care."

After driving a few miles up I-70, they took an exit and stopped at a small grocery store. They paid too much in cash for a day's worth of supplies and kept going away from the highway. They continued down the lonely back road until the unmarked turn for an even lonelier unpaved road. Even if some clever FBI agent had tailed them this far, they wouldn't be going any farther without a four-wheel-drive vehicle. The chance they could do so without Liam or Cross spotting them was about zero.

They turned off the rough road onto a patch of dirt that was barely a road at all. A few miles later, they arrived at the cabin they'd built after a profitable heist.

It didn't look like much; it was more a shack than a proper cabin. There was no electricity, but there were lanterns, a Coleman stove, and a wood-burning fireplace that kept the one-room structure warm.

They were well out of range of any Wi-Fi so along with sleeping bags they kept a supply of old paperbacks to pass the time.

They weren't ideal living conditions but where it sat on the hill, they could see anyone coming for miles. Plus, only the two of them knew about the place. Even Lindsay had no knowledge of it.

Brownstone had dug into Liam's personal life, but he doubted he'd dug deep enough to find this place.

If someone had been watching them they weren't anymore.

Lindsay

Carson pulled up to the offices of Brunson Logistics and Security. Across the street was the windowless building where they kept the trucks and, at times, the cash they distributed. The building was built like a fortress surrounded by high fences lined with razor wire and iron garage doors. A guard station with two armed guards stood between the road and both the fence and the iron door.

"They serve food here?" Lindsay asked.

Carson smiled. "No, well they might have a vending machine, but we'll get lunch afterwards. This shouldn't take long."

"Won't Gomez be pissed?"

"How will he be able to tell?"

"I figure he'll find a way to make us aware"

"He will, but if it comes down to anything but him barking, I'll take all the blame. Until right this second you thought we were going to lunch. You told me not to go in there, but I wouldn't listen. The only reason you followed me inside was to prevent me from doing something stupid."

"You don't have to take all the blame…"

"Why not? What are they going to do? Make me retire? I can walk out of here anytime with my full pension. You're not quite there yet."

Carson got out of the car and started walking briskly toward the front door. Lindsay had to hurry to catch up.

Before they stepped inside, Carson said, "Since you're here under protest, let me do all the talking, okay?"

"Sure, just don't get used to it."

The offices across the street from the fortified garage were much easier to get into. All Carson had to do was open the door. He had his badge out before the receptionist got out a word.

She looked nervous as she said, "Someone from the FBI was here yesterday."

"Yes," Carson replied, "I guess they talked to a Ms. Worth."

"She is in charge of personnel."

"I already knew that, but thanks. I need to talk to her."

"She's busy. You should have made an appointment. The man yesterday made an appointment."

"I'm sure she can make time to fit me into her busy schedule. In fact, I bet she can see me right now."

The receptionist didn't seem so sure, but she picked up the phone on the desk and dialed Ms. Worth's extension.

"Sorry to disturb you, Ms. Worth, but there are two FBI agents here to see you."

The receptionist hung up the phone and said to Carson, "I guess you would have won the bet. She'll see you now."

The receptionist hit a button under the desk and the door behind her unlocked. Carson and Lindsay walked through.

The door led to a short hallway. A portly middle-aged woman in business attire was standing in the hallway with her hands on her hips.

"Ms. Worth?" Carson asked.

"That's me," she replied.

"I'm Special Agent Carson and this is Special Agent Lane."

"I was expecting Agent Gomez. He said he'd be the liaison between Brunson Logistics and the FBI."

"He's busy," Carson told her.

"So am I, so let's get whatever this is over with."

Ms. Worth turned around and walked down the hall to the corner office. She stepped inside and Carson and

Lindsay followed. Once everyone was inside, Carson shut the door behind them.

"I hope you're here to tell me you've cleared all our people."

"No, we're not even close to that point yet."

"You should be. I told Agent Gomez I vet all our employees myself and I wouldn't hire a thief."

"No one in their right mind would, but yet they still keep finding jobs," Carson replied.

"Not with us, they don't," Ms. Worth began. Then a look of doubt crept over her face and she asked, "Are you here because you found someone?"

"No."

Ms. Worth's face morphed from doubtful to smug. "Then what can I do for you?"

"I'd like to see your upcoming schedule."

"We don't release that information."

"Even to the FBI? I could subpoena it, but it's an unnecessary hassle."

"You need to talk to Mr. Brunson."

"The owner?"

"No, his son. He's in charge of scheduling drop-offs and pick-ups."

"Is he here?"

"No."

"Where is he?"

"I don't know. He comes and goes as he pleases. He's related to the owner and that means he makes his own schedule."

"I see. Sounds like nepotism in action."

"No, I mean, yes of course being the son of the company's founder affords him some privileges, but he's actually good at his job. He's been doing it for over a decade and until last week we've never had a problem. For the record, that was not his fault. Whoever robbed that bank just got lucky."

"Long odds to pull that off."

"Long odds on the lottery, but someone wins every week. I can try to call him."

"Please do."

Ms. Worth walked over to her desk and picked up the phone. She dialed a number and waited. While the phone rang, Carson gave her his card.

She looked confused so he told her, "For the voicemail."

As predicted the phone went to voicemail. Ms. Worth left a voicemail to the younger Brunson with Carson's information.

"Anything else?" she asked.

"You sure you or someone else in the building couldn't get that schedule for me?"

"Not without that subpoena you mentioned earlier."

Carson mulled it over for a long second before he told her, "Thanks for your time, Ms. Worth. Make sure Mr. Brunson calls me back, please."

"He's got your number," she said before turning the large computer monitor on her desk so it was between her and the FBI agents.

Carson and Lindsay walked out.

In the parking lot, Lindsay said, "Are you sure you want to take no for an answer?"

"You want me to bring the power of the federal government down on that woman?"

"You could have at least made her feel you might."

"Or we get some lunch and then, since I have all their personnel files on my computer, I just look up Mr. Brunson's home address and we pay him a visit."

Lindsay

Lindsay and Carson worked until Gomez called it a day, before heading over to the address Carson pulled from the computer for Robert Brunson III.

"He said he wanted us to work to make up the time missed," Carson said before they left, "But he didn't say what to work on."

"Are you still taking all the blame when this goes sideways?"

"Of course. I'm actually looking forward to it."

They pulled into his driveway. Brunson's house was a fairly modest suburban tract home in a neighborhood that was still considered nice but was probably at the beginning of the slow decline old neighborhoods go through, as money flows to new places farther away from downtown.

"You might expect the son of the owner would do better," Lindsay said.

"You suppose he might be bitter?"

"It's happened before. It's possible he's tired of being a middle-class logistics manager and wants to move into ownership."

"So, he rips off his own dad?"

"Technically he ripped off the bank but sure. You look skeptical."

"I won't rule that out just yet, but let's see how this plays out before we put the cuffs on him."

Carson rang the doorbell. They could have called and said they were coming, but both agents preferred talking to people before they had a chance to rehearse their story.

A female voice said, "Someone is at the door."

A male said, "I wasn't expecting anybody."

"I didn't see a wife on his file," Lindsay whispered.

"He has to marry a girl before he can have her as a guest? And they call me the old-timer," Carson said with a smile.

The female voice asked, "Who is it?"

Carson held his badge up so the person looking through the peephole could see and said, "FBI. We'd like to talk to Mr. Brunson."

"FBI? Seriously?"

"Ma'am, can we come in, please?"

A deep voice yelled out, "Let them in, Steena!"

The door opened and a long-legged blonde stood in the doorway. She was wearing a man's t-shirt that was long enough to pass for a short skirt and nothing else. As soon as she opened the door, the smell of good marijuana hit both agents.

"You really FBI?" she asked.

"Be too late if we weren't," Carson told her.

"What do you mean?"

"Door's open."

"What?"

"He's giving you a hard time," Lindsay told her as she held up her badge. "Can we come in?"

"Don't you need a warrant?"

"We don't want to search the place. We just have a few questions for Mr. Brunson."

From the back of the house, the male voice said, "Just let them in already."

She didn't appear so sure.

"Pot's legal in Colorado," the voice reassured her.

She stepped aside.

Carson smiled at her after they entered. "Actually, the state of Colorado declared it legal. The federal government has not."

"Okay, so?"

"FBI is federal."

"Ignore him," Lindsay told her.

"Why don't we talk out back?" Brunson said as he appeared in the hallway. He'd put on a pair of jeans along with his t-shirt.

The FBI agents followed him to the backyard. He had a wooden deck off the back door. Carson saw the blonde follow them outside.

Brunson took the hint and said, "Why don't you wait inside, Steena?"

"Are you in some kind of trouble?" she asked.

"Of course not. It's just work stuff."

She still appeared to be doubtful so Lindsay said, "Just a few logistical questions about his work."

"Is this about the bank robbery?" she asked.

"Just wait inside. This shouldn't take long."

She nodded and headed back into the house, closing the door behind her.

"What can I do for you?" Brunson asked as he took a seat at the table set up on the wide side of the deck.

Lindsay and Carson took the chairs opposite him.

"We'd like to see the upcoming schedule. Most importantly, big cash drop-offs," Lindsay said.

Brunson frowned. "Company policy is we don't give that out to anyone outside of essential employees."

"That includes the FBI?"

"Yeah."

"Even if it could help us solve a crime where a man died?"

"Hey, I want to help, but the downside of having that information out there is huge."

"We noticed."

"That could have just been luck, them showing up right after the cash was dropped off."

"Could have been, probably wasn't."

Brunson nodded. "I can see why you would think that. Hell, if I wasn't personally involved, I'd think the same thing, but I can't see any of our guys being involved in something like this. If someone did use our schedule to plan a robbery, can you see how we might not want more of that information getting out there?"

"I can," Lindsay told him, "Which is why if you let us see the schedule, it stays with us."

"Just you two?"

Lindsay looked at Carson who nodded.

Brunson sighed. "I don't know you guys."

"We're the FBI," Carson told him.

"Yeah, so? You going to say that means you never lie?"

"We could subpoena it," Carson said.

"Yeah, you could."

"If the First National drop-off was leaked, chances are good other drop-off times were leaked as well," Lindsay told him.

Brunson shook his head. "Not at the same time they weren't."

"Why are you so sure?"

"It has occurred to me too, only about two minutes after I heard about First National. We do the schedules a week at a time and change everything up just about every time so we don't create an observable pattern if we can help it. I figured everything on this week's schedule was compromised, so the first thing I did was change everything up. It was a pain in the ass and I had to coordinate with everybody, but I got it done before the day ended. If someone really leaked this week's schedule, it's worthless now."

"Unless the leaker received the new schedule," Lindsay said.

"Possible but not probable. Crews and drivers don't have any idea where they're going until they arrive for their shift. They'd have to call during work to inform someone else."

"Has that always been the policy?" Carson asked.

"Yeah, we trust our guys, but you can never be too careful."

Lindsay felt she'd wasted all day looking at drivers and crews. She shook her head and looked at Carson. "First National was hit in the morning. Seems it'd be kind of hard for a crew to be there ready to go on a moment's notice."

He nodded. "But not impossible." Carson looked at Brunson and asked, "Did anyone inform the agent who secured the personnel files about this policy?"

"I told him myself. This the first you're hearing of it?"

"It is."

"In his defense, this policy hasn't always been as strictly enforced as it has been this week. Someone who really wanted to find out could have easily done so. Hell, they could have asked me and I would have told them."

"Did someone ask?"

"No. The guy I talked to asked me about that as well."

"Special Agent Gomez?"

"Yeah."

"You sure we couldn't see it anyway?" Lindsay asked. "We could at the least make sure no one is using it to plan robberies."

"I would if I could, but even though I'm in charge of the scheduling, I'm not in charge of anything else. He might see your point, but it'd be my ass if I gave it to you and he didn't. I like this job. I don't want to lose it."

"Who's he?"

"Dear old dad."

"He'd fire you?"

"He's been looking for a reason ever since Mom convinced him to hire me."

"How long has that been?"

"Twelve years."

"That's a long time."

"I'm good at my job."

Carson nodded. "Is he home?"

"You going to show up and ruin his evening?"

"Did we ruin yours?"

"Nah, just delayed the fun. I have to admit I am hoping you'll ruin his."

"We will do what we can, but it would be easier on all of us if we could call him. I'm assuming we'd still have to get the schedule from you?"

"That's the way it should be. It is a need-to-know basis, and he doesn't need to know, but he insists I send him a copy every week."

"It'll still save us a trip."

Brunson shrugged and stood up. "Can I get my phone?"

"You could tell me the number and I'll call," Carson said.

Brunson laughed. "I don't know it off the top of my head, but it's in my phone."

"Okay, go ahead."

While Brunson went inside, Lindsay said, "It looks like Gomez gave us the busywork."

Carson nodded. "Yeah, but someone would have had to do it. Might have been better not knowing we were working a long shot. It's better for the attitude."

"The elder Brunson isn't on our list."

"Yeah, oversight on Gomez's part."

"Could be business isn't as good as it seems."

"Always possible."

"What do you bet he has the updated schedule?"

"I'd say he does."

Brunson returned. "I took the liberty and called him myself."

Carson stared at him.

"Sorry, you can still call him if you want, but I thought why let you have all the fun?"

"All the fun?"

"I'm not the only one in the family who enjoys blondes. His new girl and mine could hang out since they're about the same age. Actually, Misty is a few years younger than Steena, so maybe not."

"Misty waiting inside?"

"No, Steena."

"What did he say?" Lindsay asked.

"He said he's leery of giving out the new schedule, but he has no problem giving out the old one if that will help."

"Both would be better."

"Sure, but he said he wanted to talk to legal first. He's afraid if he 'made it public' and another bank got hit, the company might be liable."

"We're not exactly the public."

"Yeah, and I'm guessing the lawyers will tell him the same thing. Let me have your number, and I'll set it up for you to get it the second I have it."

Carson dug a card out of the pocket of his jacket and handed it to Brunson. "Email is on there if you want to send it over."

"You want me to email the old one?"

"Could you print it? I'm still kind of old school that way."

"Sure, give me a minute."

"Of course."

"You want a beer or something while you're waiting?"

Lindsay said, "No thanks."

Carson asked, "You got like an IPA or something? I'm not a big fan of light beer?"

"Of course, I've got some Odell. I'm not much for the light beer myself."

"That'd be great."

Brunson went back inside.

"Drink on duty often?"

"Am I on the clock? Besides, I've found it's good policy to take a drink when someone is offering."

"Guess I shouldn't have said no."

"You shouldn't have for two reasons. One, beer is delicious. Two, beer drinkers automatically have a little less trust in people that don't drink."

"So, he trusts you now?"

"More than you."

A fully dressed Steena stepped onto the patio with two cold cans of Odell Elephant IPA. She handed one to Carson and opened the other for herself.

She looked at Lindsay. "You sure you don't want something? He's got other stuff than beer."

Lindsay was about to say, "I'm good," but with what Carson just told her in mind she said, "Actually, the beer sounds good."

Steena held hers out. "Have mine. I'll get another for myself."

Lindsay took it and Steena walked back inside for a minute and then returned with her own beer.

"Sorry I was being a brat earlier," she said between sips, "since we're not in trouble, this is actually kind of cool.

I feel like I'm having a beer with the girl from *Silence of Lambs* or something."

Lindsay smiled. "I'm taller."

Carson laughed and looked at Steena. "I don't remind you of any movie stars? Maybe I could be an older and fatter Brad Pitt?"

Steena shrugged. "You're too short."

Brunson returned with two sheets of paper and his own beer. He handed the papers to Carson.

"There's not much there since we only have one more day left in the week. There was only one cash drop-off on the old schedule. I circled it. Of course, no one is actually stealing that cash since I changed the drop-off time."

Carson looked at the top sheet and found the bank circled at the bottom. "Mountain Express Federal Credit Union, nine-thirty."

"The one on Colfax or the one out east?" Lindsay asked.

"Stapleton Avenue, the one out east," he replied. Carson turned to Brunson. "This is the same time as First National. Is the number at the bottom the cash amount?"

"Yeah."

"So, a bigger score than the First National."

"It would be if it was going to happen."

"Thanks. Can you get me the updated schedule when legal clears it?"

"Sure, but it might only be good for a couple of hours by then."

"Can you tell me if there is an afternoon cash drop?"

Brunson considered that for a long second. "Sure, but no details, okay? Dad is already pissed I interrupted his Viagra time with Misty."

Steena rolled her eyes.

"Hey, I didn't ask. He made it a point to tell me. Trust me, that's the last picture I want in my head."

"Same for all of us," Lindsay said. "Is there going to be a cash drop-off on the updated schedule?"

"Yeah. A big one."

"Can you talk to legal before it happens?"

"I'll try. Are you convinced whoever did First National is going to do it again?"

Carson shrugged. "If they do, I'd like to be there."

Brunson nodded. "I'll do my best to make that happen."

They made some small talk while finishing their beers and then Lindsay and Carson said their goodbyes.

"I hope he's on the level," Carson said once they were in the car, "I kind of liked him."

"Yeah, he seems okay."

"I guess you think we should stake out Mountain Express Credit Union tomorrow morning?"

"I do."

"Even if it's no longer on the schedule?"

"There's a good chance the thieves aren't aware they changed the schedule. You think Gomez will let us?"

"If we ask him? No. But we don't have to ask him."

Lindsay nodded. "It's a long shot."

"So, is finding the inside man among Brunson's employees. Besides we can bring our laptops and do some reading while we watch the bank."

"Meet there tomorrow?"

"No, that's practically the middle of the day for me. We meet at the office and leave from there."

"Sounds good."

"I will say I'm a little worried about what will happen if this long shot pays off. There will be three of them and two of us. We already know at least one of them doesn't mind shooting people. I'm a bigger target than I used to be."

"We see them and we call for backup. I'm not one for playing cowboy."

"Me neither, but if something is going down, I'm not one for sitting on my hands either."

"You want to skip the surveillance?"

"That would also be sitting on my hands. I just want to make sure we both make an informed decision about what we're getting into."

"I'm aware."

"I get it, if I saw what you saw…"

Lindsay swallowed hard. "Like I said, I'm aware. Probably more aware than most."

"Which is why I'd understand if you didn't want to jump into that aspect of the job so soon."

"I'm fine."

"You sure?"

"I just said so, didn't I?"

Carson nodded and didn't bring it up again.

Liam

"You know we could still back out?" Cross said as they drove the Buick they'd stolen a few days ago out of the garage where they'd stashed it. It was a risk using the same car, but the quick turnaround didn't give them much time to steal another one. It wasn't always easy to lift a car these days and they didn't have time to scout an appropriate target. They had snagged a new set of plates off the same model Buick to mitigate some of the risk.

"Which would mean we're driving around a hot car for no good reason?"

"Still might be the right call. The more I think about this, the more it seems wrong."

"I understand what you mean. This is a good score, but having people on the payroll to follow us around doesn't make sense either. I have to assume he's paying Tiny and Big Jim to hang out and make threats too."

"It would seriously cut into his end of the score. Unless they're working for free or he's planning on cutting us out of our end, it doesn't make sense. I guess he's paying them anyway and just had to take a break from whatever they do for him normally to threaten us?"

"Possible, but still feels wrong."

"Or he doesn't pay them?"

"How would that work?"

Cross shrugged. "It could be a common cause? Tiny and Big Jim had some prison ink, the usual white power shit. Likely for them, it wasn't just about keeping themselves alive inside."

"True believers in a cause?"

"It's not impossible. I didn't get that vibe from Brownstone or Danny, but..."

"You didn't not get that vibe off of them either."

"Exactly."

"That would actually be worse."

Cross turned a corner and they were on the street for Brownstone's bar. He stopped at the red light about a block away and said, "Last chance to back out. I can just keep driving and leave Danny standing there."

Liam considered it for a long moment before saying, "I don't know about you, but I'm in the mood to rob a bank this morning."

"It's actually a credit union."

"Shut up and drive."

Danny was standing in front of The Big Bad Bodacious Bar and Grill sipping on a cup of coffee. A duffle bag was slung over his shoulder with his gear.

Cross stopped the car and Danny got in the back seat. Once the door was shut, he drove toward the Mountain Express Credit Union on Colfax.

Rosa

Rosa waited at the bus stop and watched until Ian's bus faded out of sight.

He was off to kindergarten and she didn't have work until later that evening, giving her a solid four hours to herself. She'd considered calling Liam, but after thinking about it for a few minutes, some alone time seemed more enticing.

She didn't mind being around other people, but every once in a while, she enjoyed just being by herself. It was something she hadn't done very often since Ian was born.

Rosa saw the man in the nice suit standing by the entrance to her building. She didn't recognize him but assumed he was waiting for someone inside. She didn't care to pay much attention to him either way.

Her building had a security door. She punched in the code and it unlocked. As she pushed it open, the man in the suit put his hand on it to keep it open. It surprised her since he hadn't seemed close enough to reach it when she punched in the code. Whoever he was, he moved quickly and quietly.

Still Rosa didn't think much of it—he might have had a legitimate reason to come inside—but she put a spring in her step to put some distance between the two of them just in case.

She didn't get far before he grabbed a handful of her long dark curly hair.

She spun around and saw the large revolver at his side.

"Hey, look..." she began.

"No need to beg for your life or honor or money or anything else," he told her as he kept his foot against the door.

Rosa looked past him and saw a large man wearing a sleeveless flannel shirt lumbering toward the open door. She realized the man with the gun was holding the door for his large friend.

"Who said I was begging?" she said as she looked the man in the eyes. She didn't like what she saw.

"We're going to go back to your place and then all we'll do is wait for a phone call. After that, my friend and I go home. Are we clear?"

"Sure."

He loosened the grip on her hair as the big man reached the door.

Rosa kicked him in the groin and pushed him as hard as she could into the fat man.

She sprinted down the hall knowing if he decided to shoot her she'd be an easy target in the narrow hallway.

She considered screaming for help, but all she could see was the well-dressed man with the dead blue eyes putting bullets into anyone who dared to investigate.

His footsteps were right behind her, loud and clear. She didn't turn back to see where he was. As she reached her front door, Rosa thanked her lucky stars her keys came cleanly out of her pocket and slid into the lock with no trouble. She unlocked the door and was inside just ahead of the two men. She locked the door and ran toward her bedroom.

Before she could decide whether to go for her gun or her phone, she heard a boot kicking the door. The sound of splintering wood made her decide on the gun.

Because she had a young kid, she kept it in a locked box on a top shelf in her closet. Rosa ran to it and pulled it down.

The metal box had a combination lock. Her fingers didn't fail her and the box was open within seconds.

If the .38 revolver sitting on her shelf had been loaded, she might have put a bullet into the well-dressed thug before he reached the closet. She put one bullet into the spindle before his fist found her temple.

Rosa didn't know how she got to her knees, but the gun was still in her hand. She only had one bullet, but that would have to be enough. She snapped the spindle shut, taking another punch before she could do anything else.

She was on the floor this time and the boot that kicked through her door was on her hand. While the heel of the rattlesnake skin boots he was wearing crunched the little bones in the back of her hand, the man picked the pistol off the floor.

"Police Special. Nice gun, reliable," he told her.

"What's this about?" she asked as he took his foot off her hand.

"We're just going to wait for a phone call."

She rolled over so she was facing him and saw this time he was pointing the gun at her. "And after that?"

"That depends on your boyfriend. He does what he's supposed to, me and my oversized pal apologize for the door and the trouble and ride into the sunset."

"Sunset?"

"Just an expression. You worried we'll still be here when the kid gets home, Rosa?"

Rosa simply stared at him her mouth agape.

"No need to be concerned. This goes right and you'll still have time to get breakfast after we're gone."

"And if it doesn't go right?"

The well-dressed man smiled. "Let's just hope it does. Now, get up. We can wait in the front room. It's a lot more comfortable."

Lindsay

"I'm feeling like some breakfast," Carson declared. "Anyone else?"

Lindsay replied, "I could use some breakfast myself."

Gomez was still looking at his screen when he said, "I already ate."

Lindsay stood up and said to Carson, "You driving?"

Carson stood as well. "Sure."

They both grabbed their laptops and headed out to the parking lot.

Carson put his laptop inside the car and then opened his trunk.

"If it pays off," he said as he pointed inside.

Lindsay looked in and saw two Kevlar vests, a pair of M-14 rifles, a Mossberg shotgun with extra shells on the strap, and extra mags for both assault rifles.

Carson took off his sports jacket and put on a vest. He covered it back with a sports coat. While he was a little thicker than usual, it wasn't obvious he was wearing body armor.

"I'm not putting that on under my blouse," Lindsay said.

"Bummer, my plan to get you to strip off your top is foiled," Carson said with a smile.

"You're not funny."

"Sure I am. Keep it in the car with you. If things look like they're going to turn ugly, you can put it on," he said as he opened the back door. He grabbed the extra vest and put it on the back seat.

Lindsay grabbed an M-14 and checked the magazine. Finding it fully loaded, she set it on the floor by the passenger seat.

"It won't do me much good in the trunk," she said.

"Just make sure you put on the Kevlar before running out to engage."

Lindsay nodded.

"Hey," a voice said from behind them.

They both turned around to see Willis approaching.

"That's a lot of heavy-duty hardware. Where are you going for breakfast? Ukraine?"

Neither Lindsay nor Carson replied.

Willis smiled. "Don't worry. I won't tell Gomez. Let me guess, you got the schedule yesterday and are staking out a drop off?"

"Could be."

"Without me?"

"We've got room," Carson said.

Willis nodded and held up a finger. He walked over to his own car and retrieved a Kevlar vest out of the trunk. He put it on under his coat, picked up an HK MP-20 and checked the magazine. When he found it satisfactory, he grabbed a spare mag and joined them.

"You just keep that kind of stuff in your trunk at all times?" Carson asked.

"Yeah, don't you?"

"No, I checked this stuff out from the armory."

Willis shrugged. "Old HRT habit, I guess. Speaking of HRT, you know you two are breaking the first rule of engagement?"

"Which is?"

"Don't let your enemy outnumber you. Good thing I decided I was hungry," Willis said as he put his gear and himself into the back seat.

Lindsay and Carson got in with Carson taking the wheel.

As they pulled out of the parking lot, Willis said, "Do we have time to stop and pick up some breakfast? I actually am kind of hungry."

They had to drive across town, but they made good time so they could stop for bagels. The Mountain Express Federal Credit Union was in a mini-mall next to a grocery chain. The lot was fairly full and the store was busy. They found a parking space where they could see the Credit Union and waited.

"The armored truck would be just pulling in if the schedule hadn't been changed," Carson said.

"So, if we have the timeline right, our robbers should be just pulling in to watch," Lindsay added.

They focused on a few spots in front of the bank.

"If they think they already left, they might pull right up to the front of the bank like before, so be ready to move," Carson said.

Lindsay put on her vest and put the M-14 in her lap.

They watched a Buick sedan pull into the lot and head toward the front of the bank.

"Didn't they use a dark blue Buick Encore last time?" Lindsay said as she watched the car back into the parking space.

"It was black, but I could see how the two could be confused," Willis replied.

"Were the windows tinted?" Willis asked.

"It wasn't in the report, but that doesn't mean they weren't," Lindsay replied as she picked up the binoculars and tried to get a look inside.

"How many?" Willis asked.

"At least two; I can't see in the back seat."

"Do they fit the description?"

Lindsay lowered the binoculars and shook her head. "I can't tell with the tint on the windows."

They watched the car. No one got out.

"Are they waiting for the armored truck?" Willis asked.

"Could be."

"If they are, it'd be easier to take them down while they're all still in the car," Willis said.

Carson nodded and looked back at Willis. "Okay, this is more your thing than mine. How should we play it?"

Willis considered this for a second then said, "Give me thirty seconds to get in position and then pull up and block them in. Do it fast and hard. Get out the same way and be ready to rock and roll."

"Where are you going to be?"

"I'll come up from behind. If this turns into a firefight, do me a favor?"

"Name it."

"Don't shoot me."

"I'll do my best," Carson told him.

That must have been good enough for Willis. He took off his coat and put it over the HK and then slipped out the back door.

Carson counted slowly to thirty, took an extra second to make sure there were no pedestrians in front of his route, and stomped on the gas.

Liam

Downtown traffic didn't cooperate with Liam and his crew. They arrived at the Mountain Express Federal Credit Union a good ten minutes later than they'd planned. Cross saw a spot in front of the bank and backed in.

"I don't see the armored truck," Danny said.

"They weren't at First National for over five minutes. We must have missed them," Liam replied.

"Shouldn't we have seen them coming out, though?" Cross asked.

Liam shrugged. "Not necessarily. They could have left through the other side or even if they didn't, they could have got out before we saw them."

"Even on the road?" Danny asked.

"They could have gone the other way."

"So, the money is there?"

"Possible. They could have hit the same bad traffic we did," Cross said.

"So, do we wait and make sure?" Danny asked.

"If we wait too long, the money will be in the safe and we won't be able to get someone to open it and get out in under two minutes. If they've already been here, we need to go now," Liam said.

Cross rubbed his chin. "If the armored truck arrives while you're inside, we're going to have three more guns to deal with."

"If that happens, we're screwed, so leave without us," Liam said.

"Wait, what?" Danny asked.

Cross ignored him. "We could walk away."

Liam considered this. "Nah, I'm still in the mood to rob a bank today."

"It's a credit union."

Liam pulled his hood over his head and donned his hockey mask. "Whatever. Shut up and drive."

Cross was just about to hit the gas when a dark sedan pulled in front of them.

Lindsay

Carson slammed on the brakes and came to a stop right in front of the Buick. There was a car parked behind the Buick and cars parked on either side, leaving them boxed in.

It was good to have them trapped, but it increased the odds they would come out shooting.

Lindsay already had her door halfway open before Carson skidded to a stop, so she was out first. She hoped to get out and get her gun up before anyone in the car reacted.

She saw Willis come around the passenger side from the back holding his gun up ready to fire.

Lindsay yelled, "I need to see hands out of the windows and I need to see them now!"

No one in the car moved. Lindsay could see two white males sitting in the front. It was hard to read their faces. She still couldn't tell if someone was in the back or not.

Carson came around the side of the car, holding his pistol. "Let me see your hands."

The passenger side window came down and a pair of hands came out without a weapon.

"Everybody's hands, now!" Carson commanded.

The driver stuck his hands out of the window.

"I said, everybody!" Carson said.

"This is everybody," the driver shouted.

Willis moved along the side of the car, looking to see if anyone was in the back. He couldn't see anyone, but the tinted windows made it difficult.

"Keep your hands where I can see them," he said as he reached into the open window and pressed the button that unlocked the doors.

He pulled the back door open and looked inside.

He stepped back and said, "Clear!" and then pulled the driver's door open.

"What is this?" the terrified driver asked as he looked down the barrel of Willis's sub-machine gun.

"Why are you parked in front of this bank?"

"I'm picking up my mom."

That was the first time Carson looked at him carefully. He was barely old enough to drive.

The passenger, who appeared younger said, "He's telling the truth, look."

The passenger pointed to the front of the bank where a middle-aged woman stared at them with confusion and terror on her face.

Willis lowered his gun. "Unless this is a family operation, we have the wrong Buick Encore."

Willis felt his phone buzz. He saw it was Gomez calling and answered.

All Gomez said was, "Get to the Mountain Express on Colfax as fast as you can. It's going down."

Willis put his phone in his pocket.

"Who was it?" Lindsay asked.

"Gomez. He said to get to the Mountain Express Credit Union. It's going down."

"We *are* at Mountain Express Credit Union," Carson replied.

"He meant the other Mountain Express Credit Union," Lindsay said as she moved to the car.

Liam

The sedan blocking their way drove past and Cross pulled in front of the bank.

Liam was inside first. The guard by the door was six-and-a-half-feet of muscle. The guard saw the inside of the barrel of his shotgun and got down on the floor without being asked. He may have been built like a small truck, but no amount of weightlifting would make him immune to 12-gauge magnum pellets.

There was supposed to be a second security guard, but he was nowhere to be seen.

Danny covered the teller—like before, a young woman in her early twenties—and an older balding guy with a thin mustache who wore a bright blue tie and had a name tag reading "Devon Higgins, Bank Manager" pinned to his shirt. Devon Higgins had rolled up the sleeves on his dress shirt, ready to load the new cash into the safe.

He raised his hands above his head and said, "We're cooperating. Please don't hurt anyone."

Neither Liam nor Danny bothered to respond. While the manager and teller raised their hands, Liam took the guard's gun. He took a second to check for an ankle holster before getting to his feet and heading for the counter.

Just like before, he saw the money bags sitting on a cart getting ready to be put in the safe by the manager. It was significantly more than before. He and Danny would need to make two trips if they were going to get it all.

Two trips would mean more time. Instead of trying that, Liam said to the manager, "Bring the cart."

The manager didn't argue. He pushed the cart around the counter and stopped.

"Take it to the car," Liam told him.

Danny opened the door so the manager could push the cart through and then followed him. Liam was about to follow when one of the side doors of a small office used by loan consultants and financial planners opened.

He expected a suit-wearing financial planner; instead, he saw an armed security guard.

The guard reached for his weapon, but Liam was faster, swinging his shotgun around before the guard could clear his weapon.

The guard, upon seeing that he was beaten, stopped. Liam didn't fire, telling him, "Raise your hands."

He didn't feel comfortable disarming the guard without someone to cover him, so he stepped to the man and used an uppercut blow with the butte of his shotgun to the bottom of the guard's chin.

The guard fell back and bounced off the wall behind him before falling unconscious at Liam's feet.

Liam turned to go, but as he did, the guard he had disarmed before tackled him. Liam hit the floor with his arms pinned. The shotgun left his grip as his back hit the floor.

The guard was built like a linebacker and he tackled like one too. By the time Liam realized what was happening, the guard had pinned him down, shotgun pointing his way.

Liam was hoping the guard would let him surrender when he heard Danny say, "Drop it or this credit union is going to need a new manager."

Both the guard and Liam looked up to see Danny holding his shotgun to the manager's head.

Danny motioned to the teller who was still standing in the same spot with her hands above her head. "Probably going to need a new teller too. I ain't asking again."

While the guard was trying to figure out how to handle the situation, Liam used the side of his hand to chop the guard in the throat.

The guard clearly spent a lot of time in the weight room, but his Adam's apple was just as susceptible to a throat strike as someone who had never touched a dumbbell their entire life.

While he was trying to breathe, Liam snatched the shotgun away and jabbed him hard with the butt of the gun in the nose.

Liam got to his feet as Danny spun the manager around so they were facing each other.

"Bye, asshole," Danny told the manager.

"Pull that trigger and you're going to join him," Liam said as he leveled his gun Danny's way.

"Dude, I just saved your life."

"And now I'm saving yours. We need to go."

Danny hit the manager across the face with his shotgun and turned to the door.

Liam glanced at his watch as they hit the sidewalk. They'd been there for two minutes and forty seconds.

They could hear sirens as he and Danny jumped into the Buick.

By the time they reached the exit, a squad car had pulled in front, blocking them. Cross drove up on the sidewalk and hopped the curb. As they drove past the squad car, Liam fired out of his window, taking out the back tire.

Danny laughed. "That bitch ain't following us anywhere."

"Yeah, but his radio still works," Liam said.

Cross punched the gas and pushed the Buick to the limit.

"How far?" Danny asked. He hadn't been part of stashing the second car and didn't know where it was.

"A few blocks," Liam replied as Cross sped through an intersection against the light. Brakes squealed and horns honked, but no one ran into them as Cross took a hard left into a residential neighborhood.

They didn't stay in the residential area long. They hit another major road with no one following them, but Cross didn't slow down. He pulled into an industrial park and drove through until they came out the other side.

No one was on the road, so Cross continued to a long-abandoned gas station. They had parked the second getaway car in the back.

Cross opened the trunk from inside and the three men got out quickly. Danny and Liam grabbed as many bags as they could carry as Cross opened the trunk of the unassuming Toyota Corolla that was their second getaway car. Unlike the Buick, this car belonged to him. While it didn't look like much, none of the parts under the hood were stock. If he had to outrun somebody, he could.

It took each of them two trips to transfer all the money. They stripped off the hoodies, put everything in a garbage bag, and threw that in the trunk of Corolla as well.

Cross took out a metal pipe with threaded ends that were capped. There were wires going inside that were attached to a cheap cell phone with two wires on the outside that weren't connected to anything. He also retrieved a can of gasoline before closing the trunk. He handed the gas can to Liam and walked carefully to the Buick.

"You sure we have time for this?" Danny asked.

Liam ignored him and started pouring gasoline on the Buick.

"This car is burned for sure this time," Cross said as he placed the pipe on the front seat of the Buick. He held his breath as he tied the two loose wires together and turned the cell phone on. The bomb was now a phone call away from going off.

Liam poured some gas on the front seat even though it probably wasn't necessary and then tossed the can onto the back seat.

"Let's go," Cross said.

"About time," Danny said as he climbed into the back seat.

Cross had a police scanner in the glove compartment. He also had the Raven MP .25. He palmed the pistol and handed Liam the police scanner.

While Liam turned on the scanner, Cross put the pistol under his thigh and started the car.

There was plenty on the scanner about the robbery, but nothing to indicate anyone was in pursuit. Cross pulled out from behind the gas station. There was still no one on the road. He pulled onto the isolated road and started the pre-planned course to the freeway.

"Hey," Danny said as he retrieved his phone, "can I blow up the car?"

Before anyone could reply, a police car with sirens blaring appeared on the other side of the road, coming right at them.

Danny put down his phone and reached into the bag for his shotgun.

"Wait," Liam said as Cross pulled to the side of the road but kept the car rolling.

"How about you blow up the car now? Before he finds it?" Danny asked.

"Shut up," Liam told him.

The cruiser sped past without giving them a second look.

Cross kept driving, keeping an eye on the mirror.

"If he turns into the gas station, we're screwed," Liam said.

Cross nodded and took out his phone. He had the phone number for the bomb in his contacts so he could detonate the device with the touch of a button.

"What are you waiting for?" Danny asked. "Blow that bitch sky high."

"He might pass it by. I can detonate it from anywhere I have cell phone service. This would work better if we're nowhere near here when it happens."

"Then why aren't you putting the pedal to the metal and getting us the hell out of here?" Danny said.

"Because that will tell him we're trying to run."

"Better safe than sorry. Stomp on the pedal, dude!"

Cross kept it at the speed limit.

The cruiser slowed at the gas station.

Cross got ready to blow up the Buick.

Before he detonated the pipe bomb, however, the cruiser sped right back up again and kept going.

Cross kept it at the speed limit.

"They're going to find it sooner rather than later," Danny said. "I suggest we should still get a move on."

"They didn't find it last time," Cross said.

"That was luck."

"Exactly! We've already gotten lucky once. We shouldn't plan on getting lucky twice."

"What does that even mean?"

"It means getting pulled over for speeding right now would be bad luck, so it would just be stupid at this point to risk it. Relax."

Danny sighed and looked at Liam. "You're welcome, by the way."

"Thanks," Liam said. He considered asking why Danny was about to execute the manager and possibly the teller for no good reason but decided it didn't matter. Nothing Danny could say would convince him it was a good idea. After this, they were done doing business with Mr. Brownstone.

Danny wasn't so eager to let it go. "You weren't exactly thanking me back there. You threatened to blow my head off."

"I had my reasons. You've still got your head plus a share of what looks like a hefty amount of cash. Don't worry about it."

"I'm worrying about it."

Liam shifted in the seat so he was facing Danny and then moved his hand to the butt of the Glock behind his back. "You shouldn't. It's in the past. I'm cool with you as long as you're still cool with me."

"I'm cool with you, but I'd kind of like to know why."

Liam drew the Glock but kept it behind his back. "I'm not good with people getting shot for no good reason."

"Why?"

"It's unprofessional."

Danny shrugged. "Well, I guess you're the professional."

Liam put the gun back in the holster and turned back around. A few minutes later, they made it to the freeway.

Danny laughed. "I think we just pulled it off."

Liam ignored him. "Nothing on the scanner about finding the car. Just blow it up before they do."

"Or wait until they do and take out a few pigs," Danny said. "Or is that unprofessional?"

Neither Liam nor Cross replied. Instead, Cross pressed a number on his phone.

They were too far away to hear the explosion, but in the mirror, Cross could see black smoke rising in the distance.

"Drop you off at the usual place?" Cross asked as they left the freeway.

"No, Brownstone wants us all to go to his place. We'll do the split there."

"That wasn't the plan," Liam said.

"Sure it was."

"No one told me."

"Well, I told you now."

"Do you even understand how hot we are—?" Cross said.

"—If they knew about this car, we'd have never got this far. It'll be fine."

"I don't like it," Liam told him.

"What's not to like? You made it clear you don't want to work with us anymore. This way you can be done and everyone walks away rich and happy. If we don't show up, I can guarantee Brownstone will not be happy."

Cross and Liam looked at each other. Danny hadn't mentioned Rosa Marie or Ian, but he didn't have to.

Liam nodded and Cross said, "Alright, let's go get this done."

Lindsay

Lindsay saw the police cruiser with the destroyed back tire and the ambulance in the parking lot and feared the worst.

They made the drive over in silence but seeing the aftermath, Willis said, "We screwed up and went to the wrong Mountain Express Federal Credit Union."

"We did," Carson replied, "but we didn't screw up. We were at the one on the schedule. I triple checked."

"I checked it too," Lindsay added.

The local police had sealed the parking lot off, but Carson flashed his FBI badge and they were let through. None of the locals seemed glad to see them, so they hung back and let the police run the show for now. The Denver Robbery Homicide Division and their crime scene technicians had a solid reputation. Since the FBI would have access to everything, they found there was no reason not to let them do their jobs. All the FBI agents thought their crime scene people were better, but not better enough to make everyone wait a few hours for them to show up.

They saw Gomez standing by the ambulance watching a muscle-bound man in a security guard uniform receive treatment. Carson approached him. Lindsay and Willis stayed behind and let the two Bank Robbery vets talk among themselves.

"How bad?" Carson asked Gomez.

Gomez didn't turn from the ambulance as he replied, "No one dead."

Carson considered some follow-up questions but decided if Gomez had more to say he would.

After a long minute, Gomez said, "You three were at the other Mountain Express Federal Credit Union."

It wasn't a question but Carson said, "Yes," anyway.

"I told you that was a dead end."

"You did."

"I guess I wasn't completely right. They did hit a Mountain Express. Why were you there instead of here?"

"Brunson gave us the old schedule. He didn't feel he had the authority to part with the new one and thought it was reasonable to assume whoever acquired the schedule was working with the old one."

Gomez nodded. "Not unreasonable. You were wrong, but it wasn't unreasonable."

"Same crew?"

"Looks like it."

"But they didn't shoot anybody this time?"

"The branch manager said one of them wanted to. He also said he thought he was a dead man."

"What changed his mind?"

"Apparently the other robber threatened to do the same if he shot the manager."

"Interesting."

"Dude still gave two guards concussions, shot up a cop car, and stole over a million dollars, so he ain't exactly Robin Hood."

Carson narrowed his eyes. "What, a million dollars in cash? That's a hell of a lot of money for a routine drop off, especially for a credit union in this area. Doesn't that strike you as odd?"

"It does, but this wasn't your average drop. The credit union had some high-profile client moving liquid assets."

"Still comes across as unusual," Carson said rubbing his chin. "Who moves that kind of money without some red flags?"

"It sure did raise red flags, but the client had clearance and the credit union didn't want to disappoint one of their important clients."

They stopped talking as a man wearing a windbreaker reading "DPD" approached. Lindsay and Willis moved closer to see what he had to say.

He pointed to Agent Gomez. "You Gomez?"

"Special Agent Gomez."

"Whatever. I'm Collins, Robbery Homicide. We just got a call about a burning car behind a gas station over in the warehouse district."

Gomez raised an eyebrow. "How far is that from here?"

"Just about the right distance for our perpetrators to get there and leave," Collins said as he pointed behind the quartet of FBI agents.

They all looked back and saw the column of thick black smoke rising in the distance.

"A black Buick Encore?" Lindsay asked.

"By the time my guy got there, it was mostly a burning husk, but that burning husk could have been a Buick Encore. Be odd if someone else decided to blow up another mid-sized sedan this morning."

"So, we have no idea what they're driving?" Carson asked.

"We had an officer see another mid-sized sedan in the area before the explosion, but other than the dark mid-sized sedan, he didn't see much. In his defense, at the time he was looking for a Buick and whatever this was, it wasn't a Buick."

"That doesn't narrow it down much," Carson said.

Lindsay almost asked if it was a Toyota but held her tongue. There was no reason she should know the getaway car might be a souped-up Toyota, and she didn't want to explain that her brother was a bank robber and he had an associate with a thing for Toyotas. She made a note to look up Liam's friend Cross later.

"The officer is going to look at a bunch of pictures when he gets back to the station and see if we can narrow it down, but I'm not sure if it will do any good."

"You said explosion?" Willis asked. "There was a bomb involved?"

"Too hot to tell right now, but people reported hearing an explosion and soon after that, we found the car. I'm certain it's safe to say that it wasn't a coincidence."

"Is the officer who saw the sedan still at the scene?" Gomez asked the cop.

"Yeah."

Gomez looked at Carson. "Why don't you two go find the burning car and talk to the officer? Talk to the local bomb squad if you can."

Carson nodded and then looked at Collins. "This place have an address?"

"You could follow the smoke," Collins replied.

"I'd rather have an address."

"The place has been abandoned for years. I doubt if it has an address anymore. How about you find Ritchie Road and follow the smoke?"

Carson nodded and he and Lindsay headed for the car.

"After we do this, we talk to Brunson," Carson said.

Lindsay agreed.

Liam

Cross parked behind the bar.

"Why are you parking here? There are spaces up front," Danny said.

Cross shrugged. "Because I'd prefer this car not be seen on the street with a million dollars of freshly stolen cash in the trunk."

"It won't be in the trunk long."

"All the more reason to park in the back," Liam said. "You want people watching us unload the loot?"

Danny smiled. "That's why you're the professional, always a step ahead."

Liam opened his door. "Let's get this over with."

Cross let Danny go ahead of him. He chambered a round on the Raven and then palmed the small pistol.

Liam was about to open the trunk when Danny said, "Leave it there for now. Let's make sure the coast is clear before dragging in a fistful of evidence."

Liam thought that was a surprisingly well-thought-out idea. In his short time knowing Danny, it was the first good idea he'd ever heard. He didn't bother to tell Danny that.

This time they walked in the back door. Tiny and Big Jim were drinking at the bar, with Misty serving the drinks behind the stick. Tiny had his AR-15 hanging from a strap so it was by his hip. Big Jim didn't have an assault rifle but he had a Desert Eagle .50 that was about as long as his arm hanging on his hip like he was an old west gunfighter.

The normal trio of day drinkers were nowhere to be found.

"You guys carrying?" Big Jim asked.

"Not me," Danny said, "but I'm pretty sure Liam has his Glock on him."

"What if I do?" Liam asked.

"Come on, cowboy," Misty said with a wink, "you know the drill."

Liam slowly drew the Glock from behind his back and held it by the barrel as he approached the bar.

"Don't worry, Misty will keep it safe," Tiny told him as he stood up and let Liam step to the bar.

Misty looked at Cross. "You too, Clint Eastwood."

Cross drew his pistol with two fingers. It appeared he was trying to show he wasn't being a threat, but the real reason was to keep the Raven concealed.

He set it on the bar, slid it toward Misty, and walked over to stand by Liam.

She stopped it, said, "Thanks," and then placed the gun under the bar.

Liam set his pistol on the bar.

Misty picked it up. "This is a nice gun. I've always wanted one."

She chambered a round and casually pointed it Liam's way.

"I'd appreciate it if you pointed that in another direction," Liam told her.

"Be harder to shoot you that way," she replied with a smile.

"Is that what you want to do?"

"Doesn't matter what she wants," Tiny said, "the point is, she will if you don't cooperate."

"I feel like I'm cooperating."

"Where'd you stash your share from First National?" Big Jim asked.

"Why would I tell you that?"

"Because you wouldn't want poor Misty to deal with the mess that blowing your face off would create in Mr. Brownstone's bar," Big Jim said with a grin that showed off a serious need for dental work.

Cross said, "I doubt Misty has to worry about that."

She took her eyes off Liam and looked at Cross. "Why would that be?"

The Raven MP-25 seemed to appear magically in Cross's hand. He put his finger on the trigger and pointed it at her face.

Misty laughed. "What are you going to do with that little peashooter?"

Cross shot her through her left eye. As she fell, Liam snatched his Glock out of her hand.

Tiny was raising the assault rifle when Liam swung the Glock around. Liam shot him in the neck and chest before Tiny could get off a shot.

Tiny gave up on the idea of returning fire and instead tried to stem the blood shooting out of his neck like a fountain.

Big Jim drew his massive sidearm. The weight of the hand cannon he was sporting made him slow. He still would have beat Liam to the draw, but Cross shot him through the face. The bullet went through his cheek and knocked out a bunch of teeth before bouncing off the roof of his mouth and landing on his tongue.

Big Jim spit the hot slug out and looked up just in time to see the muzzle flash from Liam's Glock. He took two to the chest and dropped to the barroom floor.

Cross turned to Danny and took two bullets to the upper body before he could get off a shot. Cross stumbled back and tripped over his own feet as Danny turned his gun toward Liam.

Liam wasn't sure he would get his gun around in time so he leaped over the bar just ahead of Danny's bullets. Danny destroyed a few bottles before he realized all he was killing was the top-shelf liquor.

Cross crawled behind a table and chambered another round.

Danny grabbed Tiny's rifle since Tiny was lying on his back staring with dead eyes at the ceiling.

He bent over to grab it, but a bullet from Cross's Raven took off the tip of his nose. He swung his pistol toward Cross and let loose a few rounds that flew over the getaway driver.

Liam got up looking to join the fight, but Danny saw him in the mirror behind the bar and shifted his aim that way. Liam once again ducked behind the bar and once more Danny executed a couple of bottles of whiskey.

Danny fired his last bullets Liam's way and then turned and ran. Cross fired off a shot that missed and by the time Liam was on his feet, Danny was sprinting out the back door.

Liam looked over at Cross. "How bad?"

"Kevlar took most of it," Cross said, but the blood pooling on the floor below him said otherwise.

Liam stepped over Misty's dead body and hopped over the bar to chase after Danny but stopped when he saw the blood on Cross's shirt.

Instead of pursuing Danny, Liam hurried over and helped him to his feet. "Let's get out of here."

Cross pointed to the office door. "I don't think we should let Brownstone get away with this."

Liam agreed. He helped Cross to the bar and left him leaning against it.

He picked up Tiny's rifle and walked to the office door. Liam figured Brownstone would be waiting for him, probably hiding behind his desk. He started aiming low with the AR-15 and moved the gun steadily up and around as he fired. By the time the extended magazine was empty, the door and wall were shredded. Liam dropped the rifle and drew his pistol. There wasn't much door to kick in, but he did it anyway and then stepped back in case Brownstone had survived the bullet storm he'd unleashed with Tiny's rifle.

When no one returned fire, Liam went in low, keeping the Glock up as he looked for targets. There was nothing to shoot at. He checked under the desk and there was no one there either. He took a second to look at Brownstone's bull riding painting and was glad to see it was ruined.

Liam hurried out to Cross.

"Did you get him?" Cross asked.

"He's not here. Can you walk?"

"I got shot in the gut, not the leg," Cross said as he moved. He only made it a few steps before he stumbled.

Liam caught him and let Cross put his arm over his shoulder for support. They were walking out as fast as they could when the front door opened.

"You guys done with your meeting yet?" an impossibly skinny man in ill-fitting clothes asked.

Liam looked back and saw one of the day drinkers standing there and told him, "Get the hell out of here," then kept walking.

The day drinker noticed the bodies on the floor and said, "What the hell just happened here?"

Liam turned to him again. The day drinker surmised he could be the next body on the floor and ran away.

Liam figured the two-minute rule for banks was in effect here too and picked up the pace.

They reached the car and Liam helped Cross into the passenger seat.

"I don't usually let other people drive my car," Cross said weakly as Liam got behind the wheel.

"You're going to make an exception today."

"Where are we going?"

"I know a doctor who works for cash. Luckily, we've got some."

Cross laughed at that but only for a second before the laugh morphed into a cough. The cough came with blood.

After he wiped the blood from his chin, Cross said, "You need to get Rosa first."

Liam nodded and took out his phone. He punched the button to call Rosa.

The phone rang, but she didn't answer.

Liam left a message when the voicemail came up: "Get Ian and go."

He ended the call.

"Hope I didn't pull the trigger too soon." Cross said. "They hadn't even really threatened us yet."

"Why wait? We both knew they were going to."

Liam got on Interstate 25 and headed north.

"You're going the wrong way."

"No, I'm not. The Doc is this way."

"Rosa's not."

"She'll get the message."

"What if she doesn't?"

"She will."

"If Brownstone and Danny are still out there, even if Brownstone doesn't have any other people, she's in danger. You don't want to take that chance."

"We don't have that kind of time. You've lost a lot of blood."

"I had plenty to start with. You know I'm right. There is something next level messed up going on here."

Liam couldn't argue, but he couldn't let his friend bleed to death either.

"Just swing by and pick her and the kid up," Cross said as he passed out.

Liam wanted to, but he doubted he would have time to do both. A bad idea came into his head that might allow him to save Cross and make sure Rosa and Ian were safe. It was truly a bad idea, but it was the only idea he had.

Liam dug his phone out of his pocket and called his sister.

Danny

Danny pounded on the door to the big house on the Western edge of Denver. No one answered, so he pounded again.

A burly man with a clean-shaven head he'd never seen before answered the door.

"You're not supposed to be here..." he began, but then he noticed his nose and added, "What happened to your nose, bro?"

"I got shot, which is why I need to talk to Mr. Brownstone."

"That wasn't the plan. You all were supposed to call when everything was done."

"Who told you about the plan?"

"Who do you think made it?"

This caught Danny off guard. He took a second to process what he just heard and said, "You sound kind of proud of that."

"I just made almost a million dollars for the cause. That seems to me something to be proud of."

Danny took a second to look at the man's arms. He wore a sleeveless shirt to show off his time in the gym even though the weather was getting cooler. Danny spotted the skull and arrows tattoo on the inside of his forearm. He wasn't sure what 'the cause' was. Brownstone didn't talk about it much. He just knew all the people he had hanging around The Big Bad Bodacious Bar and Grill with the skull and arrows were involved somehow.

It surprised him, though, to hear the money he'd been stealing was for 'the cause'. He sure wasn't planning on giving up his share for any cause other than his own enrichment.

"You should stop patting yourself on the back," Danny told him. "Your plan didn't work."

The man looked confused.

Brownstone appeared at the door. "What do you mean it didn't work?"

"Can I come in? Just get a Band-Aid for my nose and some of that fancy bourbon you like to drink, well, also for my nose?"

Brownstone nodded and stepped out of the way.

Another burly dude was waiting in the living room. He looked just like the other man only with a blond goatee instead of a black one.

Brownstone told Danny, "Wait here," and left.

Danny hoped he was going to get the bourbon and medical supplies. Mostly the bourbon.

"This explains the radio silence," the man with the blond beard said.

The other nodded, "At least we..."

His partner put his finger to his lips and the man stopped talking.

"At least we, what?"

Brownstone came back into the room with a glass of amber liquid, some tape and gauze.

He handed Danny the glass of bourbon. "Tell us what happened."

Danny took a long sip. It was good, but he was pretty sure it wasn't the expensive stuff Brownstone drank. He drained the glass and sat down on the sofa. "What's going on here?" he asked. "What's this shit about a million for 'the cause'."

"You first, Danny," Brownstone replied.

Danny looked around the room. He didn't like the way the two weightlifters were looking at him.

He held out the glass. "Can I get another?"

Brownstone took the glass and left the room. He returned with a fresh drink and Danny started telling them what had happened.

Lindsay

Lindsay and Willis were on their way to the police station to talk to the officer who witnessed the possible getaway car when the call from Liam came in.

Lindsay almost ignored it. If he'd called five minutes earlier when they were at the scene of the burning car, or five minutes later when they'd reached the station, she would have. Since at the moment all she was doing was riding in the car while Willis drove, she took the call.

"Hey, Liam, make it quick. I'm in the middle of something."

"I need a big favor. I need you to go get Rosa and Ian and put them someplace safe, and I need you to do it right now."

"Wait, what?"

"They're in danger, and I can't get to them."

"What is this about?"

"This is about you helping me out and keeping my friend safe."

"It's about more than that."

"The part that matters isn't. Are you going to help me or not?"

"Tell me what's going on?"

"It's a yes or no question, sis."

"You're saying they are in imminent danger?"

"Yeah, as in it-might-already-be-too-late level of imminent danger, so we don't have time to discuss it. Yes or no?"

"Yes."

"She should be at home. I'll text you the address."

With that, Liam ended the call.

Willis saw the look on Lindsay's face. "What was that all about?"

"Family emergency. I hate to ask you this, but we need to make a stop on the way."

Willis looked as if he might argue, but Lindsay's face told him it might be a bad idea. Instead, he nodded. "Okay."

Liam texted the address and Lindsay plugged it into her phone's GPS.

"Hey, I know we're not friends, but is this something you want to talk about?" Willis asked.

"No—actually, yeah, but I'm not going to."

Willis pulled into the parking lot for Rosa Marie's apartment.

"Wait here," Lindsay told him, "I shouldn't be long."

Willis nodded and Lindsay got out of the car. She had no clue what she was walking into. She knew Liam wouldn't call if it wasn't potentially deadly, so she leaned back in before she shut the door. "Could you open the trunk?"

She expected Willis to ask her why, but he just shrugged and hit the lever by his seat that opened the trunk.

Lindsay picked up the Kevlar vest she'd taken off when they were at the local police station to interview the witness. She put it on and eyed the shotgun and Willis's HK but decided coming in toting an assault weapon might be a bit much since, for all she knew, Rosa and her kid were sitting around watching television.

She left the heavy artillery and entered the building.

When she reached Rosa's unit and saw the door splintered by the lock, she wished she'd grabbed the shotgun. Someone had kicked it in. Lindsay drew her pistol and kicked the busted door open.

She stepped in to see a big, bearded man dragging Rosa by the arm. Rosa was a petite woman and this guy might have weighed three hundred pounds, but he was having trouble with her. Because she wouldn't quit struggling, he drew a gun and pointed it Rosa's way.

Lindsay aimed her pistol. "Drop the weapon, let her go, and get on the floor."

He looked over at her, and Lindsay saw the teardrop tattoos on his face. She knew that could mean he'd killed somebody, but it could also mean he once had sixty bucks and a bad idea.

He saw FBI written in block letters across Lindsay's Kevlar vest. For a split second, it seemed he would do what he was told, but he neither let Rosa go nor got on the ground.

Instead, he said, "Or what?"

"I use a nine-millimeter slug to ruin that stupid tattoo on your face. You've got three seconds."

"How about you drop your gun or in two seconds I ruin this girl's face with a bullet of my own?"

"You'll still be just as dead a second later."

"You'd let me shoot this fine little piece of ass?"

"For all I know, she's the bad guy here and you were just defending your home from an intruder. Once you shoot her, I'll know for sure you were the bad guy."

The big man wasn't sure what to say to that.

Rosa Marie looked up at Lindsay. Lindsay thought she might say something about her seemingly cavalier attitude toward her taking a bullet to the face, but instead, she said, "He's not alone."

Lindsay caught some movement by the bedroom door and looked to see she was looking at the wrong end of a Colt Python.

The man holding it wasn't nearly as big as his partner but wasn't small either. Unlike the bearded man holding Rosa, he was clean-shaven and appeared dressed to go to work at a bank. He thumbed back the hammer. "You should drop your gun, miss."

"Don't do it," Rosa said.

The big man hit her on the bridge of the nose with the butt of his pistol and then quickly pointed it back at her head. "No one asked you. Just shoot the bitch."

"You good enough with that thing to stop me from getting off a shot?" Lindsay asked.

"Maybe I care about him as much as you care about Rosa Marie."

If it was a bluff, it was a good one.

The big man said, "Hey, that's not cool."

"Shut up. The adults are talking."

"Hey..."

"The real answer to your question is yes," the man in the suit said to Lindsay. "At this range, I splatter your brains against the wall before you can tell your finger to pull the trigger. Even if I can't, odds are good you'd hit the girl. Despite what you told my friend, we both know you don't want to do that. The only thing that's stopping me is I need to find out if that vest is the real thing. Are you a genuine agent of the FBI?"

"All that should matter to you is if my bullets are genuine."

"Nah, we've already covered that. The thing is, if you are actually a Fed, why are you here? I mean, is Rosa an informant or something?"

"I'm no snitch," Rosa said.

"Then why is a special agent for the FBI here?"

"I just happened to be in the neighborhood," Lindsay replied.

"Bullshit. Tell you what. Put down the gun on the floor, and we can talk about this like adults."

Lindsay didn't move. She figured once she gave up her weapon, her life expectancy could be measured in minutes if not seconds.

"How about you first?"

"And then we all just talk?"

"Sure."

The man in the suit laughed. "If you are a Fed, I know better than to trust you. Put down the gun or get your name on the wall at Quantico and your brains on the wall of this shitty apartment."

Lindsay considered if she'd rather die standing or take the long shot that somehow they wouldn't kill her anyway, probably after torturing her to find out why she was there. She was leaning toward going out on her feet, expecting that she could duck and turn and somehow put a bullet into the man in the suit before he blew her head off. Even if the odds of that happening might be lower than putting down her gun and actually having a polite conversation afterward, it still seemed like her best bet.

She was just about to move when there was a knock on the door.

A deep voice outside said, "I'm here to spread the good word of Our Lord Jesus Christ."

"Seriously?" the man in the suit said.

"We ain't interested," the big man shouted.

"I was asked to come by. I have an appointment."

"To talk about Jesus?"

"Yeah."

"Who do you have an appointment with?"

"Rosa Marie."

Without taking his eyes off Lindsay, the man in the suit asked, "Is he telling the truth?"

"Of course he is," Lindsay said, recognizing the voice. "Why would someone lie about that?"

"I was asking her."

"Yeah, it's true," Rosa replied. "Who would lie about that?"

"Rosa is busy," the man in the suit said. "Go away."

"I'd like to hear that from Rosa."

The man in the suit said, "Tell him."

Rosa said nothing.

"Tell him or I'll kill you all, including him and your kid when he gets home. Of course, I'll wait until he's had a chance to see what a hollow point .357 slug did to his momma's pretty face first."

"I'm busy," Rosa said.

"Too busy to come to the door and tell me yourself?"

"What is this guy's deal?" the man with face tattoos asked. "He must take this shit seriously."

"Go tell him," the man in the suit said. "Just remember that if you try anything, I'm killing everybody."

"Just remember the second you point that gun at anyone but me, I'm going to start killing people too," Lindsay said.

"I've got it covered," the face tattoo guy said as he let go of Rosa's arm. He kept his gun on her as she slowly walked to the door.

She opened it a crack, but before anyone could do anything, the door opened wide and Rosa was pulled into the hall.

The door flew open again and Willis in his Kevlar with his HK in hand appeared in the doorway.

Both guns swung his way. Lindsay swung and fired toward the man in the suit. She hit him in the chest, knocking him back so that his shot went into the ceiling. She fired again twice, striking him center mass with both shots and he fell back into the bedroom.

Willis fired a single shot, hitting the big man with the face tattoo right between the eyes. He was swinging his gun around to help Lindsay put bullets into the man in the suit before Lindsay finished shooting him.

"How many?" Willis asked.

"Just those two as far as I know."

Willis moved toward the man Lindsay shot, keeping his gun on him the whole time. If he moved, Willis would put a bullet between his eyes as well. The man wasn't moving, but Willis still kicked the gun away.

"Interesting family you have here," Willis said.

Lindsay didn't answer. She stepped into the hallway and saw Rosa had taken off.

She came back inside.

"Did she rabbit?" Willis asked.

"Yeah, but I am pretty sure where she's going. Her kid is in school. I'd say she's going to pick him up before she runs to the hills," Lindsay said as she took out her phone. She used Google to find the elementary school in the area.

Willis pointed to the big dead guy's arm. "That look familiar to you?"

Lindsay looked and saw the same tattoo the girl Crumbly killed was sporting.

"That can't be a coincidence."

"No kidding. What exactly is your family into?"

"To be honest, right now I'm not even sure. We need to get to this school."

"Call it in. We've got a crime scene here. Plus, I was willing to let this be your business before, but now that bullets have been exchanged, I need to know what's going on."

"Rosa is my brother's girlfriend. He said she could be in some trouble and asked me to take her somewhere safe. Turns out he wasn't exaggerating."

"No kidding. He didn't say why?"

"Nope."

"Your brother involved with militia types? Aryan gangs?"

"Not last time I checked. Not really his style."

"Rosa?"

"I don't really know her, but I doubt it. She doesn't have the right skin tone. Can we discuss this on the way to the school?"

"We've got two dead bodies."

"They'll still be dead when we get back."

Just then, they heard the hiss of air brakes outside the window. Both of them had the same thought. They moved to the window and saw the yellow school bus across the street. A car pulled up next to the bus and stopped in the street. Rosa got out and went around the bus. A few seconds later she was dragging Ian behind her and tossing him in the back seat. They both watched as she drove away.

"I guess we don't need to go to the school," Willis said as he took out his phone.

"Did you get the plate?"

"Yep, calling it in now."

Lindsay nodded. While he was calling, she walked over to the dead man in the suit. She rolled up the sleeve on his right arm and found the same tattoo.

"Let me guess," Willis said, "he's got one too."

Lindsay nodded and then turned to Willis. "You saved three lives. Thank you."

Willis shrugged. "Just doing my job."

"I'd say you did more than that. What made you come in?"

"The whole thing just felt wrong, you know?"

"Because it was. Very perceptive. And how did you know her name?"

"I was curious so I followed you in and listened at the door. I wasn't expecting it to be a hostage situation."

"You were spying on me?"

"Yeah. I've been trying to get into the spirit of being an investigator since I'm no longer HRT."

"Normally I might complain, but in this case, I'm going to thank you."

"You could thank me by telling me what this is really about."

"As soon as I find out, I'll tell you. Why don't you call this in and I'll call my brother and get some more details."

Willis nodded.

Lindsay headed to the bedroom to make the call but stopped when Willis said, "Hey."

She turned and he asked, "Are you okay?"

"Yeah, the closest I came to getting hit was your bullet whizzing past me to hit the big guy."

"I don't mean that."

"Then what?"

"I'm familiar with your record," he said as he pointed to the man in the suit. "You've never killed anyone before."

Lindsay almost told him that wasn't true but that shooting was not on her record. It was similar in that it also involved her brother, but no one but Liam knew about it and she planned for it to stay that way.

"I guess it hasn't hit me yet. Are you okay?"

"I've killed people before. I was actually hoping when I switched to Bank Robbery my killing days might be over."

"That sounds like the answer is no."

"No, I'm fine killing that bastard. I'm not so happy about the fact I'm so good with it though."

Lindsay nodded. She knew the feeling, but she couldn't tell him about it.

She entered the bedroom to call Liam.

Liam

There wasn't much to see on the road except barbed wire fences and acres of brown grass. Cross had been sleeping for a while and Liam was sure he'd stopped breathing more than once. He considered biting the bullet and dropping him off at a regular hospital but was sure if Cross could answer, the answer would be no.

There was no way the police wouldn't connect his gunshot wound with the bloodbath at The Big Bad Bodacious Bar and Grill. Cross had been to prison once and he'd made it clear he never wanted to go back.

Liam told himself he was doing this for Cross, but the fact was he knew if the law got a hold of him, it would be hard for Cross to keep Liam's name to himself.

At last he saw the small sign saying 'Veterinary Clinic' at the end of a long dirt road. Liam took the turn and drove to Doc Deaver's place.

He parked around the back of the double-wide trailer because Deaver's operating room for both people and animals was in the back of the house.

Belinda, Deaver's long-time assistant, met Liam in the driveway. He'd always wondered why a raven-haired beauty at least fifteen years younger than Deaver lived with him in the middle of nowhere. She was dressed in scrubs and, except for the old leather gun belt with a chrome revolver hanging at her hip, looked just like a nurse.

"You get my text?" Liam said as he approached the passenger side door to grab Cross.

"Yeah, you're lucky the guy with the horse canceled," she said as she pulled on a pair of rubber gloves and walked over to help Liam get Cross out of the vehicle.

They helped him into a white room and put him on a stainless-steel table.

Belinda looked at Liam. "Help me strip him down."

Doc Deaver was by a sink in the corner of the room, washing up. He turned and moved toward Cross.

"You know if he dies, you still owe me the money," he said as Belinda cut away his shirt.

Liam nodded. "Is he going to die?"

Deaver shrugged. "It might not be worth your money."

"Do what you can. There's more in it for you if he makes it."

"Cash, up front."

"Get started and I'll go get it."

Deaver nodded and started examining Cross.

"Looks like the bullet passed through him. Good news. We just have to stitch him up and get him some new blood."

Deaver looked at Liam. "What are you waiting for?"

"To see how much to get."

Deaver looked at the gun Liam was now holding and began stitching Cross up.

Liam was going to watch the entire process, but his phone vibrated. He looked to see who was calling, hoping it was Rosa. He saw it was his sister and made his way out to take the call.

"Are they safe?"

"I guess."

"I guess? What the hell do you mean, 'I guess'?"

"I mean, most likely. My partner and I rescued her from a couple of thugs who most definitely meant her harm, but while we were at it, she ran away."

"What about the kid?"

"She had him when she ran."

Liam sighed with relief.

"Why is an anti-government militia trying to hurt your girlfriend and her kid?"

"Anti-government militia?"

"Don't play dumb."

"In this instance, I'm not playing. Why would you say they were an anti-government militia?"

"Tell me why they were after Rosa? Did it have something to do with you?"

"I asked you first."

"They had a distinct tattoo that might be related to a domestic terrorist organization."

"Might be?"

"I was kind of hoping you could confirm it. It would make it easier to track the rest of them down."

"I have no idea about that. I really don't."

"Why were they after Rosa?"

"They didn't tell you?"

"They can't tell anybody anything right now."

"I can't say I'm sorry to hear that."

"You really don't know who they were?"

"No."

"What kept you from rescuing Rosa yourself?"

"I'm out of town."

"You sure it wasn't the bank robbery this morning?"

"Someone robbed a bank this morning?"

"Yeah, was it you?"

"No."

"Where are you at?"

"Can't you ping my phone off a cell tower and find out?"

If she'd thought of it, she could have set it up, but she hadn't. "You're just talking to me right now."

"Which 'me' am I talking to? My sister, Lindsay, or Special Agent Lane of the FBI?"

"They're the same person. You need to listen to me, Liam. If you're mixed up in this and the recent bank jobs, I can't protect you. I'm your sister, but I'm also an FBI agent. People have been killed over whatever this is. I can't be your sister about this. Do you understand?"

"Doesn't have to be that way, and we both know it."

"That was a one-time thing. Your free pass from me is over."

"Keep in mind that works both ways. You want to be an agent and only an agent when it comes to me? Then I have to look at you like anyone else who gets in my way."

"Like the guard at First National?"

"I am not sure what you're talking about."

"Someone is still after Rosa. If you can tell me who they are..."

"Rosa is no longer your problem. Thanks, sis. I owe you one."

"How about you pay me back by telling me what's really going on?"

Liam hung up.

Liam was about to go back inside when Belinda met him at the door.

"Good news," she said. "He's no longer leaking and we're pumping brand new blood into him as we speak."

"Is he going to make it?"

"No guarantees, but I like his chances. Good thing for him Doc waived his cash upfront policy."

"Probably a good thing for everybody. Wait here."

Liam strode over to the car. He opened the trunk with the lever by the driver's seat. He peeked inside the trunk and couldn't believe what he saw. There was not a single bag of cash inside. The bag of clothes and shotguns that would implicate them were right there, but other than a single hundred-dollar bill they must have dropped, all the money was gone.

"Damn!" he said louder than he meant to.

"What's the problem?" Belinda asked.

Liam drew his gun and turned to face her, holding the gun at his side. "Someone ripped me off."

Belinda's hand moved toward the gun on her hip.

Liam shook his head. "Don't be stupid. You think I'd be standing here if I hadn't already won one gunfight today? How many have you won?"

Belinda moved her hand away from the gun. "Someone stole your money? Something to do with that gunfight?"

"Yeah, there were more of them than I expected."

"Tell me how's that my problem?"

"I have the money. It's just not here. Give me an hour."

"That's not the way we work."

"Give me an hour and I double the fee. Don't and the best you get is what I have in my pockets, which ain't shit," Liam said as he tapped the gun against his leg to remind her it was there. "More likely all you get is lead."

"Doc won't like it."

"I wouldn't expect him to. You've got my friend's life in your hands. I've got no reason to want to screw you."

"We won't just let him die, no matter what you do, and you know it."

"If you know you well enough to know that then you should know me well enough to know I'm going to pay you."

Belinda thought about this for a long moment before she said, "Go get our money. You have an hour."

Liam slammed the trunk and hurried to the driver's seat. He had enough from his share of the First National Job to pay Doc Deaver with some left over. That didn't mean he was going to let Brownstone get away with stealing his share from this morning's heist.

He pushed the Toyota to the limit as he sped down the country road, even though the trunk was still full of evidence.

As he drove, Rosa called.

"Rosa?" he asked.

"Yeah, you owe me an explanation."

"And you'll get one, but first, do you remember how to get to the cabin?"

"Yeah, I think so, but this car won't make it. That road is too rough."

"Dump your car. They're going to be looking for it anyway. Take the Jeep. There's a key in a magnetic box by the right tire."

"What Jeep?"

"The black one Cross and I have parked on the bottom floor of the parking garage off Fifth Street. You can't miss it."

"How are you going to get there? If they're looking for my car, they're looking for yours too."

"Let me worry about it."

"How about you meet us at the garage? We can go together."

"I have something I have to do first. You're going to have to trust me."

There was a long pause before Rosa asked, "How long do I have to stay there?"

"There's no cell phone service out there, so tomorrow drive to town at noon and get some lunch or something. If you don't hear from me, go back to the cabin."

"I don't like the sound of that."

"Me neither. I'm sorry, Rosa, I have to go."

Liam hung up before she could protest. He didn't have to hang up, but he didn't want to discuss over the phone the fact he was probably going to kill some people.

Danny

There was a long silence after Danny finished telling his tale.

Danny broke it, asking, "Can I get another bourbon?"

Brownstone got up and for a second Danny thought he was going to fetch him another drink, but instead of doing that, he looked at the twin with the blond goatee and said, "Go check it out."

"The place has got to be crawling with cops."

Brownstone shook his head. "If the cops were there, I'd be the first person they called. It's my bar."

"You think I'm lying?" Danny asked.

Brownstone ignored him. "If Danny is right, we need to clean it up."

"Why would I make that up?"

Again, they ignored Danny. The twin with the dark goatee said, "I told you not to leave that shit to them."

"Would you have preferred them to screw up the money? I trusted you with the important part and you got it done."

"Should have let us do it all."

"We're going to have to do it all now anyway."

"What are you talking about?" Danny asked.

Brownstone looked at Danny. "Don't worry about it."

Danny shook his head. "How about that bourbon?"

"You're coming with us," the dark-haired twin said. "If we have to clean up three bodies, you're helping."

Lindsay

The moment Liam hung up, there were cops yelling, "Freeze!"

It seemed the gunfight had got someone's attention. The cops weren't impressed with their FBI credentials and both Lindsay and Willis ended up in a jail cell while the locals tried to piece together what just happened.

It wasn't long before they could hear Gomez from the cell they shared.

"Why are two of my agents locked up in your jail?"

They couldn't hear the answer. Judging from Gomez's, "I don't care which cell they're in" response, the cop must have tried to explain they weren't in the jail but a special holding cell segregated from other prisoners.

This was correct, but it didn't matter to Gomez.

"You think the fact he's so mad at them will make him less mad at us?" Lindsay asked.

"Unlikely. We might be better off staying here."

Soon after, Gomez, flanked by a police captain and a pair of plain-clothes detectives, appeared in front of their cell.

"The police say they arrived at the scene of a shooting, with two dead bodies, and you two weren't very forthcoming."

"How so?" Willis replied. "We told who shot them."

"Actually what we were more interested in is why," one detective retorted.

"They were trying to shoot us."

"You put out a BOLO on the tenant," the other detective said. "How does she fit into this?"

"We wanted to ask her why the men in her apartment wanted to shoot us."

Gomez gave Willis a harsh look. "I'd like the answer to the next question myself."

The detective obliged, asking, "Why were you there?"

Lindsay stood up. "Tip from a CI that she was in some kind of trouble."

"And this took priority over your current case?"

"At the time, it seemed reasonable we could do both."

Before Gomez could reply, Willis said, "If we hadn't gone there how do you think it would have worked out for Rosa Romero?"

No one had an argument for that.

"Are you going to let them out or what?" Gomez asked.

"I don't like you guys coming down here and turning my city into the Wild West," the captain said.

"It was the Wild West before we got here," Gomez said.

The captain signaled to someone back at the jail entrance and the barred door opened.

Willis and Lindsay stepped out.

"Any ID on the two dead men?" Willis asked.

"Yeah, big guy is an ex-con named Able Brently. His smaller partner dressed like an accountant was Bob Lee Hanson who worked as, you guessed it, an accountant."

"If you're wondering," the other detective added, "both men owned multiple guns, but none of the guns at the scene were registered under their names. Or anyone's name."

"Interesting company."

"Able listed his employer as The Big Bad Bodacious Bar and Grill, a little dive downtown that caters to the redneck and urban cowboy crowd. Probably a bouncer. It looks like one of Bob Lee Hanson's clients was The Big Bad Bodacious. So, they may have met there."

The other detective added, "We've been trying to reach the owner, without success."

Lindsay nodded. "Any connections to right-wing militias? Aryan gangs?"

"Able did a lot of time where joining an Aryan gang is kind of mandatory for a guy with his complexion, but nothing other than that in his file. We don't really have a file on Bob Lee. Why?"

"Could be nothing, but they both had a tattoo that might be a gang thing."

"Might?"

"Yeah."

"Why does the FBI Bank Robbery Unit care about those assholes?" the detective asked.

"It was her old job," Gomez explained, jerking his head at Lindsay.

"Since we couldn't reach the owner, we thought we might stop by The Big Bad Bodacious Bar and Grill. You three want to tag along?"

Lindsay looked at Gomez, expecting him to say no, but he said, "Go on, while you were locked up, Carson talked to the officer."

"And?"

"A dark blue Toyota Corolla. Not exactly get-away car material."

Lindsay nodded as she tried not to let recognition show on her face.

"Whatever this is, get it over with," Gomez said, "and then get back to helping us catch the bank robbers."

Danny

"No way am I putting them in my Bronco. It's a bloody fucking mess," the blond goateed twin said as the three of them stood by the bar, looking over the carnage.

"You can always get the inside cleaned," his brother suggested.

"You want me to take a car covered in evidence to a car wash? Even if I was that stupid, there's no guarantee they'd ever get the smell out."

"We can clean it ourselves."

"So, my ride becomes the meat wagon and I get the pleasure of cleaning up the mess?"

"I'll help."

"How about instead we go get your truck then? It's not like the bed has upholstery."

"You want to drive through town with three dead bodies in the bed? Out in the open?"

Blond Goatee didn't have an answer to that.

"Even if that was doable, we have time problem. It's a kind of miracle that no one has discovered this yet."

"Pretty sure the day drinkers saw it all," Danny said. "They're just too degenerate to call it in."

The twins ignored him. "I understand why you don't want to put them in your new Bronco, but we've got to do something, sooner rather than later."

"How about we wrap them in plastic or something?" Danny suggested.

"You got any plastic?"

"No, but maybe we could go to Home Depot and buy some."

"Not the worst idea," the dark-haired twin said.

"How far to the nearest Home Depot?"

"Wouldn't have to be Home Depot, could be Ace or Lowes," Danny suggested.

"Whatever, how far?"

Danny didn't know.

"Unless there's one around the corner, we have the same problem we have with going to get his truck."

"There isn't one around the corner."

"Then how does that help?"

Danny shrugged.

"Well, we've got to do something."

Before anyone could respond, they heard a voice outside the front door say, "If you ask me, you guys shouldn't go in there."

The blond Corsica twin mouthed, "Cops?"

His brother shrugged and drew his gun.

Lindsay

The detectives arrived at The Big Bad Bodacious Bar and Grill first but waited by the door for the two FBI agents.

Before they entered the bar, a disheveled man wearing ill-fitting clothes intercepted them.

"If you ask me, you guys shouldn't go in there," he said.

"Why not?" Lindsay asked.

"There's some bad shit going on in there. I can't say for certain they're done."

The older of the two detectives flashed his badge. "What kind of bad shit are we talking about?"

"Never mind. Just be careful," the man said as he turned to walk away.

Willis put his hand on the man's shoulder, but he pushed it away and started running.

"Should we chase him?" Willis asked.

"You can," the older detective said as he drew his gun.

Everyone else did the same. Willis kicked open the door and was the first to step inside the bar.

They noticed Tiny's big body first. Because they had no idea if the shooter was still around, they quietly checked the rest of the bar, finding Big Jim and Misty.

"The bum was right, this is some bad shit," the older detective said after they determined the only people inside were corpses.

Lindsay put away her gun and knelt next to the big dead man. She lifted his arm and rolled back the sleeve.

"Look familiar?" she asked.

"What the hell have we stumbled into here?" the younger detective asked.

"Not sure yet," Willis said as Lindsay checked the arm of the short man, "but so far everybody has the same taste in tattoos."

"We'd better call this in," the older detective said.

He and his younger partner stepped outside.

Lindsay went around the bar. Underneath, she saw a woman's purse. She put on her rubber gloves and carefully opened it. Inside she found a wallet and in the wallet, there was a driver's license belonging to a woman named Misty Blevins.

Except for the blood and the missing eye, the driver's license photo matched the dead woman behind the bar.

She looked over at Willis. "Where have I heard the name Misty before?"

"A Clint Eastwood movie from the seventies?"

"Nope, that's not it," she said as she checked the dead woman's arm.

"Same tat on the inner arm?" Willis asked.

"Yeah."

Willis pointed to the floor. "There's a blood trail leading out toward the back. Did anyone check outside?"

Lindsay shook her head and they followed the blood trail. They paused to take in the destruction of the office.

"Did you find any blood inside the office?" Lindsay asked.

"Not a drop."

They reached the back door and saw the blood trail kept going.

They followed it outside to an empty parking spot.

"Someone walked out." Lindsay said.

Willis nodded. "You need to tell me what your brother's into."

"I honestly have no idea."

Willis stared at her for a long second before saying, "But you could make an educated guess."

Lindsay sighed. "After we lost our parents, we ended up in foster care. He didn't take to it very well and because of our age and potential issues…"

"Potential issues?"

"Our parents were killed gangland style."

"Hey, I didn't know…"

"I don't advertise it."

"They catch anybody?"

"Yeah, a hitman by the name Sokolov. He didn't do it on his own though. Why he did it or who he did it for was never determined."

"Damn. That's messed up but…"

"You wondering what that has to do with this case?"

"Sorry, that sounds harsh…"

"But we've got enough dead bodies to form a basketball team."

"Well, yeah."

"He ran away and found a family friend to take him in."

"Him but not you?"

"I didn't want to go. Uncle Corey is a criminal. I never understood why my parents were friends with him. Liam looked up to him, but I never liked him. I used to think he was somehow responsible for what happened."

"You don't anymore?"

"I don't know what to think. I used to think he was some big-time outlaw because he liked to present himself that way, but once I joined the Bureau I looked into him the way only an FBI agent could. As far as I could tell, he's a small-time thief with no connections to the type of men who could hire Sokolov."

"Don't get mad, but did you look up your parents?"

"Yeah, nothing to link them either. Trust me, I looked hard. By that time I'd already assumed they were into something shady. Otherwise, why would they be targeted? I found nothing. The point is, my brother grew up with a crook. My parents might have been clean, but my brother isn't."

"And they still let you into the Bureau?"

"His record is clean. Until right this second I've told no one, even…" Lindsay began but stopped herself. It was bad enough Willis knew about Liam; he didn't need to know she had a relationship with Agent Logan.

"Logan," Willis finished for her.

Lindsay glared at him with her big eyes.

He shrugged. "Sorry, it wasn't exactly a secret. Unlike your brother possibly being the new Al Capone."

"I wouldn't call him the new Al Capone, but between Crumbly, Logan, and Liam, I probably should update my resume."

"Why?"

"You serious? My own brother is mixed up with a terrorist organization I was investigating!"

"You said his records are clean though?"

"Yeah, but..."

"But you know he's not, and now so do I. Until he does something to cross the line, that can stay between us."

Lindsay wasn't sure what to say.

"In the meantime, this seems like a case for your boyfriend. Whatever is going on here, I doubt it's connected to our bank robbery. If your brother's dirty, it'd be better if someone else took him down."

Lindsay nodded. "Thanks."

"You're welcome."

"This is the second time today I had to thank you."

"Yeah, I think I could get used to it. You want to call Logan?"

"You were on the case too. You do it."

"You don't want credit? We might have found something huge. Whoever these guys with the tattoos are, we can say they're into something—and it looks like that something was going to involve Dennis Crumbly, who wanted to do some kind of major damage."

"Meaning the tattoo group probably was down with doing some major damage and, unlike Crumbly, they might still be around."

"Assuming there's more than six of them, yeah. If you didn't notice the tattoo, this still might be flying under our radar. This kind of thing might get you back into Counterterrorism."

"You saved my life; you take the credit."

"I don't want to go back to HRT. I quit on my own, remember?"

"Once I make this call, it's out of our hands. We go back to chasing bank robbers."

"I'm looking forward to it."

Lindsay made the call.

Danny

Danny said, "Screw this," and headed for the back door.

The twins could have stayed and shot it out with whoever came through the door, but they both saw the logic in Danny's decision. They followed him out the back.

They were parked across the street watching as the police crime scene technicians descended on The Big Bad Bodacious Bar and Grill.

"Now what?" Danny asked.

The twins looked at each other and then Blondie said, "We go back to Brownstone's place, I guess."

They made the drive back and Danny ended up in the study with a bourbon in his hand while the others went into another room to talk. Part of him wanted to be there to hear what they were saying, but most of him was glad to be left out of it. It was tempting to go home, but they'd told him to wait.

He was on his second drink when the Corsica twins came back into the study.

"Where's Brownstone?" Danny asked.

"He's talking to the cops. Don't worry he won't say anything."

Danny nodded.

Blondie asked him, "You still have all of your cut from the first job?"

"Most of it. Why?"

"You work at The Big Bad Bodacious. They're going to talk to you, maybe search your place."

"Why? How would they know I was there?"

"They wouldn't, but you have a record, right?"

"Yeah..."

"So, you're going to be the prime suspect right away. You know how cops are."

Danny couldn't disagree.

"Where's the money?"

"Why?"

"Because we need to make sure the cops don't find it. If they find out you robbed the banks, they might start looking into Brownstone, which would be bad for a whole bunch of people."

"It's safe," Danny replied.

"Given that I'm one of those people it'll be bad for, I'm going to need more than your say so."

"Let me worry about that."

"We're just trying to help."

Danny thought about that for a second. He didn't believe it.

"What did Brownstone mean when he said you two took care of the money?" Danny asked.

Blondie smiled. "While you were inside the bar, we took the money."

"You ripped us off?"

"No, of course not. If we were ripping you off, why would I tell you? We were making sure the thieves didn't somehow get away with it."

Danny wasn't sure what to say.

"Your share is waiting at our stash house, where it's safe," Blackie said.

"Be better if we put it all in one place," Blondie added.

"How about we go get my share now?"

Blondie shrugged. "Sure, but do you have a safe place to hide it? Especially with the cops about to come down on you hard over a triple murder?"

Danny was thinking about that when Blackie said, "You didn't stash the money at your place, did you?"

Danny did, but he didn't want to admit it.

"You know that's the first place the cops are going to look."

Danny had no answer to that either.

"So, let's get your money, and then we'll get your share from this morning, and you can put it at our stash house or find your own place. What do you think?"

Danny didn't like it, but he couldn't think of a reason to say no.

Liam

When Liam arrived back at Doc Deaver's place, Belinda greeted him with a view of the wrong end of her gun.

"If you didn't bring money, this won't be much of a fight."

Liam got out of the car. He'd managed to get to his stash, grab it, and get back in under an hour. Since he was early, he'd taken the time to count out Doc Deaver's share and keep the rest in the hiding place in Cross's trunk. If they'd used the false bottom in the first place, he could have saved himself some trouble.

"It's on the seat."

"I should shoot you anyway."

"Bad business shooting potential customers."

"Yeah, you are the kind of guy people like to shoot. Stand back and keep your hands up."

Liam did as he was told. She retrieved the paper sack from the front seat and glanced inside.

"Can we trust each other now?"

She thought about it for a second. "Let me count it first. In the meantime, you can visit your friend."

"He's alive?"

"Not only that, he's awake…or he was. He really wanted to talk to you. Refused some quality drugs just so he could have the opportunity."

She took the bag and went inside the main house. Liam walked toward the door leading to Doc Deaver's operating room.

Cross didn't look good and the multiple tubes sticking out of his body didn't make him look better.

He couldn't sit up, so Liam moved to where he could see him by just turning his head.

"Belinda said you wanted to talk to me."

"I couldn't remember if I told you about Danny."

"What about Danny?"

"I know where he lives. Did I tell you that?"

"No."

"Huh, I would have sworn I did. Good thing I stayed awake to ask you."

"Where does Danny live?"

"Actually I am having second thoughts about telling you where he lives. We've got the money."

"Get over it and spit it out," Liam told him. He didn't have the heart right now to tell him about the money.

Cross winced. "I am not really sure…"

"You didn't turn down quality drugs and go through all this pain for nothing."

"Yeah, that's a good point. Besides, that punk shouldn't get away clean. Stansfield Apartments, unit 219. As far as I can tell, he lives alone."

Liam nodded.

"You got it?"

"Yeah, Stansfield Apartments, unit 219."

"Good, get the Doc. I'm ready for the drugs."

Deaver must have been listening, as he walked into his operating room and went straight to the I.V. with the clear fluid. He twisted a plastic piece at the bottom of the bag and a painkiller meant for horses slowly seeped into Cross's bloodstream.

Before he passed out, Liam asked, "How did you know?"

"They followed us so I had to follow them."

"Brownstone too?"

"Didn't have time. I probably should have followed Brownstone instead."

"Nah, you did good."

Cross managed a crooked smile. "I did, didn't I?"

Liam waited until Cross was sleeping before asking Deaver, "How long can he stay here?"

"I've got no appointments the rest of the week, but that can change."

"Can I get twenty-four hours more?"

"Yeah, I can do that."

Liam looked at his watch. "Alright, see you in twenty-four hours unless I can get back sooner."

Lindsay

After Lindsay called Logan, he took over. They left the crime scene to the locals and the Counterterrorism Division. Lindsay stuck with her story that the call to check on Rosa came from a confidential informant and Willis said nothing to dispute it.

Even though they'd already put in a full day, after a short dinner break, Lindsay teamed back up with Carson to go talk to the younger Brunson. Once again, they didn't call ahead.

His girlfriend, Steena, answered the door.

"He's out back," she told them. "He thinks you're going to arrest him."

"Did he do something we should arrest him for?" Carson asked.

"He says no but thinks this morning's robbery will be blamed on him."

"Someone leaked it," Carson told her.

"You really think it was him?"

Lindsay asked, "What do you think?"

"I think if he was going to do that he'd tell me."

Lindsay nodded. She knew that just because Steena believed Brunson wouldn't lie to her didn't mean he wouldn't. In her experience, the people who thought their significant other was always honest were often lied to the most.

Steena stepped out of the way so they could go find Brunson the third.

He was just finishing a joint when they spotted him on his deck.

Lindsay sat down across from him. Before she said anything, she saw Steena watching from the door and remembered something.

"You here to arrest me?" Brunson asked.

"Not yet," Carson told him.

"What was your dad's girlfriend's name?" Lindsay asked.

The question caught Brunson off guard. "Uh, why?"

Carson looked at her. He was thinking the same thing.

"Because I asked you."

"Misty."

"You said she looked kind of like Steena."

Brunson looked back. "Did I?"

"Yeah."

"They're the same type, tall blondes, but…"

"Misty had more tattoos, more…"

"Tits," Brunson finished, "though I'd bet she paid for those, or someone like my old man did. What does that have to do with anything?"

Lindsay took out her phone and found the picture she had taken of a dead man's tattoo. She held it up so Brunson could see it. "She have a tattoo like this?"

"I'm not sure. We don't hang out much. My dad and I aren't that close and I couldn't care less about his latest girlfriend."

"But you've met?"

"Yeah, he got it in his head that we should act like father and son, and we all met for drinks. It didn't really go well. Honestly, I think he wanted me to see he had a younger stripper girlfriend like it was some kind of contest."

"She was a stripper?"

"I assume at some point."

"She's a bartender," Steena said as she stepped outside. Everyone looked at her.

"She told me that night we got together for drinks."

"At The Big Bad Bodacious Bar and Grill?" Lindsay asked.

"How'd you know?"

Lindsay looked at Carson. "I think I know how the schedule got out."

"If you say so."

"We need to go see the elder Brunson, and I think we need to do it now."

"Sure, you want to tell me why?" Carson said.

"No."

"No? Why not?"

"If I'm wrong, it won't matter, and I really hope I'm wrong."

"So, I'm not going to get arrested?" Brunson asked.

"Not yet," Lindsay replied.

Carson added, "Unless you want to be."

"I'm good."

Before they left, Lindsay called Willis.

After he picked up, she asked, "Still working?"

"Yeah, why?"

"If you're in front of a computer, could you run a background check on Misty Blevins?"

"The dead girl at the bar?"

"That's the one."

"I thought we passed that on to your boyfriend?"

"He's not my boyfriend, and this might be related to our case after all. Can you do it?"

"Done! Ran the names of her dead friends too. You want it all?"

"Yeah, I do."

"I'll send it right now."

As they got in the car, Carson asked, "So, you and Agent Logan are no longer a thing?"

"Does everyone know about that?"

"You work with professional investigators. The bigger question is why did you think no one would find out?"

"I'm going to take the fifth on that one."

Carson drove and Lindsay read up on Misty, Big Jim, and Tiny.

Lindsay

Robert Brunson II lived in a much bigger house than his son, in a gated neighborhood with security at the gate. The badge got them through the gate without issue, though they were sure the guard called Brunson to let him know they were coming.

A short fat bald man answered the door in a tailored suit that didn't quite hide the extra weight around his midsection.

"Agents Carson and Lane," Carson told him as he flashed his badge. "We're here to talk to Mr. Brunson."

"I'm his lawyer, Mr. Cochrane. Mr. Brunson already talked to Agent Gomez."

"I'm not Agent Gomez," Lindsay replied.

"Mr. Brunson has requested any meeting between him and law enforcement be conducted by appointment. Agent Gomez respected this request and I suggest if you want continued cooperation, you do the same."

"I'm actually here to talk to Misty," Lindsay told him.

"Who?"

"Misty Blevins. I believe they are in a relationship."

"I don't know anything about Mr. Brunson's personal relationships. It's not my business."

"Perhaps you better educate yourself. Unless there is another bartender named Misty Blevins working at a downtown bar called The Big Bad Bodacious Bar and Grill, this is about to become your business."

"Why is that?"

"Someone shot her in the face."

A hand appeared on the portly lawyer's shoulder and moved the lawyer out of the way. An older, shorter version of the younger Brunson appeared in the doorway. Somehow, this version had less gray hair and fewer wrinkles around the eyes and forehead, yet despite the Botox and hair dye, he still looked his age.

"Did you say something happened to Misty?" he asked, looking anxious.

"Do you think something happened to Misty?"

"She hasn't been answering my calls. She was supposed to come over and have dinner."

Seeing the look of worry on the old man's face made both FBI agents pause. He didn't look like he was going to take the news very well.

"Was I hearing things? I thought you just said someone shot her in the face?"

Carson sighed. "You thought correctly."

Brunson seemed to go into shock. He tried to speak, but no words came out of his mouth.

Anticipating some kind of accusation, the lawyer said, "I've been with Mr. Brunson all afternoon."

"I don't think your client shot her," Lindsay replied, "but we do have some questions. Can we come in?"

Brunson barely spit out the words, "Is she okay?"

"No."

He looked as if he was going to cry but wiped the tears building in his eyes and somehow composed himself.

"Can we do this later? My client is obviously distraught..."

"It's probably going to get worse," Lindsay told him, "probably better if we get it over with."

"What do you mean?" Brunson asked.

"I'd prefer to tell you inside."

Brunson took a second before saying, "Alright, come inside. My lawyer isn't going anywhere, so..."

"We're not out to get you, Mr. Brunson."

He seemed to believe her. He and the lawyer walked away. Carson and Lindsay followed.

"I'm still confused. Were you right or wrong?" Carson asked Lindsay as they followed Brunson and his lawyer.

"Right."

"And that's a bad thing?"

"Yeah."

"Why?"

"Things just got very complicated."

Before Carson could ask more, they reached Brunson's den. He and the lawyer sat down in easy chairs while Carson and Lindsay sat down on the sofa.

"When did this happen?" Brunson asked.

"Either this morning or early afternoon."

"I tried to call her around eleven, and she didn't answer. How did this happen? Where was she?"

"The Big Bad Bodacious Bar and Grill, downtown."

Brunson put his head in his hands. "I told her to quit that stupid job. Was it a robbery?"

"That is yet to be determined," Lindsay replied even though she knew the cash register was full.

Brunson took a second to regain his composure before asking, "Tell me you got the scum that did this."

"Not yet."

"Then why aren't you out looking for them instead of here talking to me?"

"Because that's not my job. I work Bank Robbery."

"What does she have to do with that?"

"Maybe nothing. Am I correct that the only people with the updated schedule for cash drop-offs were you and your son?"

"You still think someone in my company was working with the scum who robbed the banks?"

"Hard to get that lucky twice," Carson told him.

"I thought we were talking about Misty."

"We are. It was a yes or no question," Lindsay told him.

"As far as I know. Yes."

"He would email them to you?"

"Correct."

"Did Misty have access to your computer?"

Brunson paused. "What are you asking me?"

"Another yes or no question."

"She was here a lot and the computer is here all the time, but being in the same room doesn't mean she had access."

"Password protected?"

"Of course. Are you accusing Misty...?"

"I'm asking," Lindsay replied.

"Then the answer is no. She was an angel."

The FBI agents didn't bother replying.

"Did my son put this idea in your heads?" Brunson asked.

"Why would you think that?"

"He never liked her, called her gold-digging white trash. He thought she was going to steal his inheritance—as if I was going to leave that slacker jackshit anyway."

"No, your son never suggested it," Carson told him.

"Speaking of gold-digging white trash, have you looked into the slut that's living with him now?"

"Actually," Carson said, "yeah."

Brunson looked surprised.

"She came up clean."

"There's always a first time," Brunson replied.

"Do you want to know what we found out about Misty?" Lindsay asked.

"There's nothing you could tell me I didn't know. She didn't lie to me."

"Is her past why you didn't disclose her as a significant other when we asked after the first robbery?"

"Careful, Agent Lane," the lawyer said. "That sounds a lot like an accusation."

"She didn't need to be punished again by you people for mistakes she made in her teens," Brunson added.

"Which mistake was that?"

"I'm guessing the one you're thinking of was the liquor store in Arizona. So what? She dated an idiot and he tried to rob a liquor store. They punished her for it and still, she made something of her life. I'm not about to stand for you two jack-booted government thugs bad-mouthing Misty. I wouldn't have tolerated it when she was alive and I sure as hell ain't tolerating it when she's no longer around to defend herself."

"I believe my client is asking you two to leave."

Carson stood but Lindsay stayed seated.

"You heard the lawyer," Brunson told her.

Lindsay stayed seated and pointed to the laptop on the table by Brunson's chair. "Is that yours?"

"Why?"

"I'd like you to check on the login history."

"Get out of here."

"I can get a search warrant. Considering the circumstances, it won't be very hard."

"Then I'd suggest you do it."

"You run a business that requires people to trust you with enormous sums of money."

"Tell me something I don't know…"

"You're not the only armored truck company around."

"Again, tell me something I don't know. Get the hell out."

"How will your clients feel when they hear the FBI is serving a search warrant on your property in connection with two robberies? One that left a man dead."

Brunson had nothing to say about that.

"If Misty was just an upstanding young woman caught in the wrong place at the wrong time, there shouldn't be any log-ins other than those made by you. I don't care about anything else."

"You can check that?"

"Yes."

"I recommend you do not let her do this," the lawyer said.

She looked at the lawyer. "Do you really think I can't get a warrant?"

He stayed silent.

Brunson picked up the laptop and opened it up. After logging in, he stood up and handed it to Lindsay. Carson sat back down.

"You are to look at nothing but his log-in history," the lawyer said.

"She can look at whatever she wants," Brunson replied.

Lindsay saw the computer used the Windows operating system, so she went to the events viewer and found a list of all the logins for the device over the last two months.

"Anyone other than you ever use this laptop?" she asked Brunson.

"No."

She scrolled down to week before the first robbery and found what she was looking for.

"You don't log in at two-thirty in the morning very often."

"I work for a living. All I'm doing at two-thirty in the morning is sleeping unless it's the weekend and even then, I don't make it to the wee hours of the morning very often."

She turned the computer to face him. "Someone logged in at 2:32 on a Tuesday."

Brunson found a pair of glasses on the table where the computer had been sitting. He stood up and took a closer look.

"That's not the only Monday you logged in after two."

Brunson sat back down. "The machine must be acting up."

"What day does your son send the schedule?"

"You don't have to answer her," the lawyer said.

"If I don't, they'll just ask him. He sends the schedule on Monday."

"Was Misty over that night?"

"That proves nothing."

"It's a yes or no question."

"Yes."

"Can I check your email log-in history?"

Brunson sighed. He looked defeated.

"I recommend against it," the lawyer said.

"Go ahead," Brunson said.

Lindsay went to the email log-in history and found the day of the late-night log-in.

She turned the laptop so he could see it again. "Is this your email address?"

"No, it's Misty's. This explains it. I let her use my computer to send an email before."

Carson smiled. "Let me guess, you gave her your password to log on."

Brunson didn't reply.

"Don't answer that," the lawyer said.

This time Brunson didn't.

"Did you save your email password on this device so you don't have to log in every time?"

Again, Brunson didn't answer.

Lindsay pointed at the history. "Someone logged into your email at 2:35."

Brunson stayed silent.

"If it wasn't you, who was it?"

Brunson shook his head. "She wouldn't do that to me."

Lindsay closed the laptop. "Because she loved you and told you everything, even the other arrests?"

"What other arrests?"

"I'm not going to go into details, but you need to realize she might not have been who you thought she was."

Brunson looked away.

Lindsay got up and joined Carson.

"What now?" Brunson asked.

"I know what I need. Hopefully, there's a trail to the rest of them."

"If people find out I let this happen…"

"You've been cooperative, reluctant but cooperative. If someone finds out, it won't be from me."

Brunson nodded and watched the detectives walk away.

Before they got to the car, Carson said, "You know there's no way this doesn't get out."

"Sure, but it won't come from us."

"Too bad she's dead. I would have liked to talk to her about this."

"Me too, but maybe she left a trail."

"Can we follow it in the morning? I'm exhausted." Carson slumped his shoulders.

"You know, as of tomorrow I'm going to be on desk duty…unless they suspend me. It's probably why Gomez let me go out and chase leads. He knew I'd be shut down tomorrow."

"I hadn't thought of that. I'm still tired as hell, though."

"Me too, now that you say it."

"Tired people make mistakes and with this case, I feel like the mistakes might be fatal."

Lindsay couldn't disagree.

"I guess you're going to need to trust Gomez and myself to follow up."

Lindsay didn't like that part but couldn't dispute it. At least Carson seemed to know what he was doing and even though he wasn't friendly, she was coming around on Gomez as well.

Liam

Liam found Danny's apartment without a problem. He considered kicking in the door and coming in shooting, but after listening for a few minutes and hearing nothing, he figured the odds were high that Danny wasn't home.

Instead of kicking in the door, he got back into the car and drove home. He spent some time circling the neighborhood to make sure none of Brownstone's thugs were watching his place. He'd done the same thing when he had gone back earlier to get the money for Doc Deaver. It was better to be safe than sorry.

Just like earlier, he went in with a pistol in his hand and spent a few minutes making sure no one was waiting for him inside.

The lock pick set that Uncle Corey had given him for his thirteenth birthday was in the closet. He put it in his pocket and headed toward Danny's apartment.

Liam spent a long few minutes listening for any sign Danny was home before he used his lock picks to open both old locks on the door and entered the apartment. The entire process took him under three minutes. Considering the age and quality of the locks, he was disappointed it took him so long and vowed to put in some practice if he got out of this mess alive.

Danny's place wasn't big; just a studio apartment that looked like it used to be a hotel. Liam still came in with the gun raised looking for targets since Danny just might be really quiet.

Since Danny was not home, Liam sat down on the couch and tried to think about what to do next. The easy answer was to wait for Danny to arrive. Then get him to spill what was going on beyond just a couple of bank robberies and put him out of his misery. Since Danny wasn't home yet, Liam spent a few minutes searching the place.

Danny had hidden his share of the cash from First National under a false bottom of his top drawer in a grocery bag along with a loaded Glock 17 sitting on top of the money. The stacks of bills still had the bands around them from the bank. Liam rifled through them and saw he was at least a stack worth short, a grand.

He'd told him to wait before spending any of the cash, but wasn't surprised Danny hadn't listened. Liam considered taking it with him. He figured Danny owed him.

After thinking it over, he decided to leave it for now. He could take it with him after he and Danny had a conversation. Just to be safe, he took out the magazine, thumbed out the bullets, and put them in his pocket.

Liam peeked out from the window of the second-floor apartment. He had a good view of the parking lot. He could also see Cross's Toyota that he'd driven in. That meant Danny might see it as well. If he was going to wait for him, he needed to move the car.

Liam left the door unlocked and went down to the Toyota. As he was walking, he got an idea. When he reached the car, he found some rubber gloves. He opened the trunk and took out the bag of clothes and guns from that morning's robbery.

He took it all back to Danny's apartment.

He'd worn gloves when putting on the clothes and handling his shotgun. Even his shell casings had never been touched by his hands. He was fairly certain Cross had taken the same approach. It would still be a tremendous risk since law enforcement seemed to find new ways to extract DNA and fingerprints.

With this in mind, he took a minute to separate what he and Cross wore from what Danny was wearing. Since they'd all worn different-sized hoodies, it wasn't that hard. The hockey masks were all the same size, so Liam went into Danny's dresser and found a shirt to wipe one down.

He found the shotgun Danny had used. He was glad they'd each used different guns so they wouldn't be confused. Liam put the hoodies, masks, and guns that he and Cross had used back in the bag and put the rest under Danny's bed.

Liam checked the window and then left with the stuff.

Carrying so much evidence was making him nervous as hell, so after putting it in the trunk, Liam drove to a grocery store nearby.

He pulled around back and no one was there.

Grocers locked their dumpsters to keep homeless people out of them, but padlocks were easier to pick than outdated deadbolts. Liam picked the lock and dumped the trash bag full of evidence inside. He closed the lid and locked it back up without anyone noticing.

All the evidence but the stuff implicating Danny would hopefully be on the way to the dump before the week ended. Liam found a parking space for the Toyota in the parking lot of the grocery store and walked back to Danny's apartment.

He was about to enter the parking lot when he heard a car slowing down behind him. It was probably nothing, but he put his head down and kept walking, using the mirrors on cars parked on the side of the street to watch the vehicle.

It wasn't easy looking into rearview mirrors on the move. Mostly he didn't see anything until he passed a truck with an extra big mirror. That and the hitch on the back made it clear the owner hauled trailers of some sort. Liam got a good view of a brand-new dark green Ford Bronco turning into the parking lot for Danny's building.

Liam didn't figure Danny to be the type who could afford a new car like that (especially given he hadn't touched most of the money from the robbery yet). He kept walking. When he reached the corner, he dared to look back.

He was glad he'd taken the overly cautious approach as he saw Danny exit on the passenger side. Liam moved so he was shielded by a parked van and watched as Danny was joined by two big dudes with shaved heads and long goatees. One of them reached under the seat before he closed the door, grabbed a big pistol, and put it in his pocket. Liam guessed it was a .45, either a Colt or a Kimber. The big dude used the front of his tank top to cover it up.

Danny didn't look glad to be there. Liam watched them go into the building with Danny leading the way and the two men behind him.

With them inside, Liam stepped out on the street and crossed, heading the other way. Taking Danny by surprise when he walked into his place could be done with only a marginal amount of risk. Barreling in and taking on two more armed men changed the odds considerably.

The evidence he'd stashed wasn't exactly well hidden, and it would give away that he'd been there. Part of him was glad he'd left the cash where he'd found it since he had a feeling Danny might check that out sooner rather than later. If his gut was right, the two men were there to take Danny's share from First National. If so, that meant he was just as much of a patsy as him and Cross.

What Liam didn't want was for them to get away with it. For the second time that day, he called his sister.

Lindsay

Despite being truly tired, Lindsay was having trouble relaxing. First she spent forty minutes on the treadmill at the hotel workout room and then put in fifteen doing a lightweight workout.

After the workout, her body was tired, but her mind was still working. A long, hot shower didn't help. To make matters worse, Logan called while she was working out and again while she was in shower. If he was calling about the sudden connection between her new case and her old one, she would be glad to talk about it, but given the time, she doubted that was what he had in mind.

She considered it might not be a bad thing but changed her mind. It was bad enough being the secret girlfriend, but now it seemed she'd been demoted to booty call. She'd had to accept one demotion when they tossed her from the Counterterrorism Division, but she didn't have to accept this one.

She didn't call him back.

Knowing her mind was unlikely to let her relax anytime soon, Lindsay decided she needed some help to slow everything down. She put on a t-shirt and a pair of jeans and headed to the hotel bar.

She was only mildly surprised to see Willis sitting at the bar nursing something amber on ice.

"I'm not the only one who needs to drown my troubles this evening?" she asked as she sat down next to him.

"I guess not. Be careful, it's a bad habit to get into."

"I don't plan on having too many more days like today."

He raised his glass. "I've said that before myself, yet here I am."

The bartender was the same man behind the stick as the night before. He recognized Lindsay. "Jack and Ginger tonight?"

Before she could answer, Willis interrupted, "I don't think it's been a fancy cocktail type of day. Get her what I'm drinking. Get me another and put them both on my tab."

"You don't need to buy me drinks," Lindsay told him.

He finished the drink in his hand in one big gulp before saying, "Oh, don't worry. You're buying the next round."

"Who said I'm having more than one?"

"If you're here for the same reason I am, you're having more than one."

If she was being honest, she couldn't tell him he was wrong, but she still didn't like him buying her drinks. She knew that for a lot of men, buying a woman a drink came with certain expectations. If she was looking for that, she could have let Logan have his booty call.

"If not, you can get me another time," Willis added.

Lindsay didn't like it, but the bartender was already pouring bourbon from the top shelf over ice.

"Woodford," Willis told her as the bartender put a glass each in front of them.

Lindsay took a sip.

"You like it?"

"Not bad for bourbon. I'm more of a Tequila gal."

"It grows on you."

"We'll see."

Lindsay's phone buzzed. She looked at the screen, figuring it was Logan again, but it was a number she didn't recognize. She decided to answer.

"Hey, remember me?" Liam said.

"This is a different number than before."

"It's a different call."

"You calling to turn yourself in?"

"No…"

"How about telling me what the hell is going on?"

"If you want your bank robber, head on out to the address I'm about to text you."

"What are talking about?"

"I suggest you hurry. I don't know how long they're going to be there."

Liam ended the call.

"What was that?"

"My CI telling me where the bank robbers are."

Willis put down his drink. "Seriously?"

Instead of answering, Lindsay looked at her phone and saw the address Liam had sent. It wasn't very far away. She called Carson anyway.

Carson picked up immediately. "What's up?"

"A CI just told me the location of the bank robbers. I'm texting it to you now."

"How reliable is the information?"

"Reliable enough that someone needs to check it out."

"Been a long day. I'll pass it on to Gomez."

After giving him the information, she looked over at Willis.

"You coming?"

"Coming? You passed on the information…"

"Yeah, but I'm still going. Are you coming or not?"

Willis looked at his drink and put it down without taking a taste. "We'll take my car. I have all the tactical gear."

They geared up in the hotel parking lot.

Just as Lindsay finished putting on her Kevlar vest, a figure came out of the darkness.

She had her hand on the gun on her thigh when Logan said, "I've been trying to reach you."

"I know."

"We need to talk."

Lindsay motioned to the Kevlar vest and the pistol holstered at her leg. "I'm kind of busy."

"Butting into my case?"

"No, trying to solve mine."

Logan looked over at Willis, who was geared up and ready to go, and then back at Lindsay. "We still need to talk."

"Okay, but I've got to go."

Lindsay climbed into the passenger seat while Willis got behind the wheel. Logan opened the back door and got in behind Lindsay.

"What are you doing?"

"Coming along. I'm still an FBI agent too."

"When was the last time you were in the field?" Willis asked.

Instead of answering the question, Logan said, "I thought you were in a hurry?"

Willis started driving.

Danny

Danny stopped in the doorway.

"What's your problem?" the blond twin asked.

Danny shook his head. Something felt wrong about his apartment, but he couldn't put his finger on what it was. He decided not to worry about it since he had other problems. He was sure the Corsica twins were going to rip him off.

The worst part was, he was pretty sure they were doing so with Brownstone's approval.

"What are you waiting for? Get the money and let's get out of here."

Danny went inside and, without bothering to turn on the lights, went straight for the money. He was relieved to find it all still there. Even better, his gun was still in the bag on top of the cash.

He had it in his hand when he felt the cold steel on the back of his head.

"Sorry, kid. If it makes you feel any better, the money was never going to be yours in the first place."

Danny took a deep breath. "If I hand you the money, do you let me walk away?"

"Of course."

Danny was pretty sure the other twin suppressed a laugh.

"Then can you take that gun off the back of my head?" Danny asked, trying to sound more scared than he was. He was scared but just like when he was robbing the banks, part of him was excited. Just like the banks, this was an opportunity to put a bullet in a fellow human being and to Danny there was no better feeling than pulling the trigger when his gun was pointed at someone.

"I don't have the money yet."

"I'm going to turn around now to give you the money. Don't shoot me."

"No problem."

Danny dropped the money bag and spun fast with the gun in his hand. He swung his free arm around to knock the gun away and partially succeeded. Blondie's shot carved a groove through the side of his head, shearing his right ear in half.

Danny put his gun in Blondie's face and pulled the trigger, but nothing happened.

For a long second, the two of them stared at each other in disbelief. Blondie had seen the barrel of the gun line up with his face and seen the hammer strike what he figured was a bullet with his name on it. He couldn't believe he wasn't dead. Danny couldn't believe it either.

Danny snapped out of his trance first when he saw Blackie pulling a sub-machine gun out from under his coat. He shoved Blondie into his brother just before Blackie pulled the trigger. Instead of putting a bullet in Danny, he blew out the window above the kitchenette.

Danny scooped up the bag and ran out of the apartment.

The brothers untangled and gave chase.

When they reached the hall, Blondie drew his own MAC-10 and pointed it, yelling "Cut him off!"

Blondie followed Danny while Blackie went in the other direction.

Lindsay

"Lindsay..." Logan said from the back seat.

Lindsay didn't bother to turn around. "I don't think this is the time nor the place."

"Why would you say something like that? I'm talking about you trying to get back into Counterterrorism..."

She turned around this time. "Who said I was trying to get back?"

"You connected your current job with your old one on your second day."

"I reported what I saw. I figured you'd want to know."

"The girl with the tattoo was collateral damage."

"Was she?"

"Until I have proof otherwise. Yes, she was."

"I have five bodies with the same tattoo who were not collateral damage."

"Are you sure it's the same? Plenty of similar tattoos out there, that don't mean anything. It's possible the girl's was just similar."

"Looked the same to me," Willis said.

"So says the other agent looking to get back into the Bureau's good graces."

"I don't want to go back to HRT," Willis told him. "I volunteered to transfer."

Logan didn't know what to say to that. Just then, Gomez called Willis and Willis answered with his Bluetooth so everyone could hear.

"I'm going to give you an address."

Willis recited the address before Gomez could say more.

"How did you know?"

"It was Lindsay's CI. We're staying at the same hotel."

There was a pause as if Gomez wanted to ask more, but he simply asked, "I suppose you two are on your way?"

"The information is time sensitive."

"I'm already coordinating with the locals for tactical support. I'm on my way as well. Don't do anything until I get there. You've already surpassed your quota for shootouts today."

"No problem."

Gomez ended the call. Soon after, they pulled into the parking lot for the Stansfield Apartments.

"Perhaps the best way to avoid another shootout would be to go back to the hotel," Logan suggested.

"No one asked you," Lindsay replied as she scanned the second floor of the building. The number would put the unit somewhere in the middle of the row, but she wasn't sure where or even if they were looking at the right side of the building. Only one unit in the row had the lights on.

"What were you two doing together when your CI called?" Logan asked.

"Having a drink," Willis replied before Lindsay could tell him it was none of his business.

Before Logan could follow up, Gomez pulled up next to them, facing the other way so he and Willis could talk.

Both men rolled down their windows.

Gomez saw Willis was wearing his Kevlar. "I thought I told you the locals were going to handle the heavy work?"

Willis shrugged. "No one ever tells bullets."

Gomez seemed to find that acceptable. He noticed Logan in the back seat. "What's he doing here?"

"I needed to talk to Agent Lane."

"She's in my crew now. While she's working, leave her alone."

"Excuse me?"

"If you wanted to talk to her during work, you could have kept her on your unit instead of sending her to me."

Lindsay looked at Logan and for a second she could see it on his face. It was clear that if it wasn't for him, she'd still be working Counterterrorism. It was only there for a second before he regained his usual poker face. But it was enough.

She was about to say something when a flash of light in a second-floor unit followed by the sound of breaking glass interrupted her. The light flashed again and then the room stayed dark.

"Muzzle flash?" Willis asked.

"I think so," Lindsay replied.

Both agents got out of the car.

"He said to wait," Logan called out. "You don't even know if that's the same apartment." But Gomez was getting out as well.

Willis had the HK up and ready and Lindsay was holding her sidearm as they approached the building.

Willis looked over at Gomez. "You're not wearing a vest. It would be better if you wait by the car."

Gomez drew his gun but nodded in agreement.

Before he could go back, a young man holding a grocery bag in one hand and a gun in the other burst through the door and stumbled into the parking lot. He fell on his face but quickly got back to his feet.

"Freeze!" Willis told him. "Hands where I can see them."

The young man looked up and saw the wrong end of three guns. He stopped but didn't put his hands up.

"They're going to kill me," he said.

"Who?" Lindsay asked as she moved to get a better look at him. She noticed his shirt over the shoulder was covered in fresh blood. The blood was coming from the side of his head and his nose had a bandage across it that wasn't stopping the bleeding very well.

Before he could answer, a shot rang out and the young man's head exploded. He slumped to the ground as a big man holding a big pistol in one hand and a MAC-10 appeared at the door. The grocery bag spilled over, dumping bundles of money on the ground. The trio of FBI agents ignored the money and focused on the gunman.

All three FBI agents yelled, "Drop the weapons!"

Instead of dropping them, the big man pulled the triggers.

Even with the rapid-fire capabilities of the MAC-10, he only got off two shots before Willis put a bullet in his head. Lindsay fired twice and hit him both times in the chest before he fell, even though he was dead the second Willis's nine-millimeter slug pierced his brain.

Willis moved toward the bodies and Lindsay looked back to see Gomez on the ground.

She was moving to Gomez when Logan shouted, "Look out! Behind you!"

Lindsay spun and got low, but if the second man with a sub-machine gun had targeted her, she'd have taken some bullets.

Instead, he swung his gun at Logan. They exchanged gunfire, but the bullets that found flesh were not fired from the FBI agent's gun. Lindsay fired twice but rushed her shots. Both bullets found their target, but neither was enough to put him down. He swung his gun her way, firing on full auto.

She pulled the trigger twice more, but she caught at least two slugs herself. Their impact had her on her back. She looked up to see the man with the Mac-10 still wasn't down. She tried to raise her gun, but her arms didn't respond very well.

The big man dropped the empty MAC-10 and drew a pistol.

Lindsay looked back and saw Willis had dived for cover when the man sprayed bullets their way. He was scrambling to his feet, but she wasn't sure he would get up in time.

She looked around and saw Gomez sit up and double tap the gunman in the chest. This time, the shooter fell and stayed down.

She and Willis remained ready with their guns raised, waiting for more targets. They did so for what seemed like a long time, though it was less than a minute.

Lindsay tried to sit up, but Willis put a hand on her shoulder and told her, "Stay down, ambulance is on the way." He took her hand. "You're going to be okay."

Lindsay couldn't help thinking this was exactly what he would say to someone who was not going to be okay. She tried not to think about that and instead asked, "Logan?"

Willis shook his head as the sound of sirens filled the air.

Sometime while they waited, Lindsay lost consciousness.

Lindsay

Lindsay woke up in the hospital. She saw Willis sitting in the chair next to her bed reading a book. She realized she was alive and heavily medicated and then fell asleep again.

Later she woke up and found herself just as alive but not nearly as medicated. She tried to sit up and was glad to find she could.

She looked over at Willis. "You've been here the whole time?"

He shrugged. "Nothing better to do. I've been suspended pending the investigation."

"I suppose I've been suspended too?"

"Not yet. They wanted to make sure you lived first."

"Speaking of which, what are my chances?"

"From what the doctors told me, you're good. Broken ribs and some superficial wounds. The vest did its job."

"I passed out."

"Not from blood loss. When you fell, you bounced your head off the sidewalk and gave yourself a severe concussion."

"I'm here because I fell?"

"Yeah."

"Kind of embarrassing."

"You fell because you took two slugs from a MAC-10, so it's not that embarrassing."

"Gomez?"

"He took a bullet to the thigh and one to the love handles. The doctors feel good about his chances."

"He saved my life."

"He's down the hall. You can thank him later."

They sat in silence for a long time before Lindsay said, "I wouldn't mind knowing what the fuck just happened."

"Me neither, but I think the local cops put together a plausible scenario. You remember the cash the first guy dropped?"

"Kind of."

"You want to bet on where that came from?"

"Only if I get to bet the credit union."

"You'd lose that bet. First National, and before you ask, they didn't find any money from the Mountain Express job. Danny must have stashed it somewhere else."

"Who's Danny?"

"Danny Danielson was the name on the lease. He was in the system, did some time for sticking up a liquor store in his teens."

"He have an arrows and skull tat on the inner forearm?"

"Nah, Iron Cross on the left shoulder and double D design on the right. Apparently, he wasn't in the club with the other seven dead people."

"Seven?"

"The two dead guys who weren't Danny Danielson had the same tattoo. The detective at the scene said, if he didn't know better, he'd think we were just going around shooting people with that tat."

"So, without the money, are we looking at two different crews?"

"Unlikely. They found a shotgun, a black hoodie, and a hockey mask. The shotgun is the model that killed the guard, and the hoodie matches the footage from the security cameras. Ballistics is working to confirm that we found the murder weapon. You want to guess where Danny Danielson worked?"

"The Big Bad Bodacious Bar and Grill?"

"Bingo."

"How about the other two?"

Willis shrugged. "They're not yet identified."

"That strike you as odd?"

"Yeah, but it's only a matter of time. The working theory is Danny and Misty hatched the plot after Misty started seeing Brunson. Since she had the tattoo, she probably hooked up Danny with the unknown dead men."

"Then tried to rip him off?"

"Or died when her friends tried to muscle in on the score. Danielson was running for his life with the bank money. Looks like his partners double-crossed him. It happens."

"So Danny killed the men at the bar?"

"It's possible."

"How is Rosa involved?"

"That one is still a mystery. One we might never get the answer for. This case is about to be closed, at least for us."

"Seriously?"

"We have three dead men at an apartment your CI said contained the robbers. One was literally caught holding the bag, and we have two bank jobs with a three-man crew. See where this is going?"

"This was the crew."

"Could be. That kind of thing happens. If it did, we just solved our first case."

Lindsay nodded. "Doesn't feel solved."

"Yeah, not exactly a big win."

"I got Logan killed."

"No, you didn't. It was his choice to come along."

"If he hadn't yelled at me…"

"It wouldn't have made any difference."

"No one asked us to be there. If we'd sat it out…"

"Then Gomez would have been there by himself. He'd be dead and the bank robbers—well, two of them, anyway—would be still running free. Sorry, you can't make this your fault."

"It was my brother that called. He set this whole thing in motion."

Willis considered this for a moment. "He passed on information, information that was spot on, by the way."

"The brass will want to know about him."

"He's a confidential informant. He should stay that way."

"He's a crook."

"We found the bank robbers and he wasn't one of them. Your brother is in the clear."

"Is he? He's involved somehow."

"He knew about it, and he did what a responsible citizen does and informed law enforcement."

"No one who knows my brother uses the words 'responsible citizen' to describe him. He's more than just a witness, and we both know it."

Willis sighed. "You're probably right, but if you tell anybody he's the CI, you're going to be out of a job."

"I guess that's fair."

Willis shook his head. "I don't think so. Neither does Gomez. You already helped solve a major crime—"

"—Because my brother is a crook!"

"You found the connection between Misty and Brunson Sr. without him. We, mostly you, would have found these guys without him. You're good at this, and you can handle yourself in a gunfight. Getting yourself fired because you're related to an asshole would be a waste."

"I can't ask you to keep that secret."

"You're right but I can decide for myself."

Lindsay looked him in the eye. "You're being awfully nice to me."

"I'm a nice guy."

"When we first met, I didn't think you liked me."

"I didn't, but you're growing on me."

"Like a fungus?"

"Yeah, like a fungus."

Both managed a smile. Lindsay's faded quickly.

"You know, Logan fucked me over."

Willis wasn't sure how to reply.

Lindsay wiped away a tear. "The sad thing is, he really thought he was doing me a favor."

"How so?"

"He thought if I was out of the unit, we could be together openly. For such a smart guy, he had some blind spots."

"Everybody does."

Lindsay

Lindsay was back at her hotel when her phone buzzed. She didn't recognize the number and while it could have been a telemarketer or even a wrong number, she knew it was Liam.

"Hello," she said as she took the call.

"Just thought I'd call and make sure you were okay. The news said you were shot."

"I was, but I'm fine."

"Sorry..."

"You should be."

"I also read where you'd solved the case. You should be thanking me."

"I would have gotten it done without you and fewer people would have died."

"Maybe. Maybe not. Either way, you can stop thinking I did it."

"Is that why you called? You wanted to see if you're still a suspect?"

"No, I wanted to see if you were doing okay."

"I'm fine. I've got a few new scars and bruises, but otherwise, I'm good."

"You had a concussion."

"How did you know about that?"

"I have my sources."

Lindsay let that go. "How's Rosa?"

"She's fine."

"She with you?"

"If she is, it's by choice."

"You know this was more than just three assholes robbing banks."

"Do I?"

"I think you do. It's why Rosa hasn't come home."

"Glad to hear you doing okay."

"Tell me what this is about. Let me take them down."

"As far as I know, this was about three assholes robbing banks. My gut feeling says the people robbing those banks thought the same thing. That's the truth."

"There has to be more."

"Probably is. If I knew what it was, I'd tell you."

"I wish I could believe you."

"I'm still your brother."

"And you're still a thief."

"And you're still an FBI agent."

Lindsay wasn't sure what to say to that.

"There's something else I wanted to talk to you about," Liam said.

"What's that?"

"I heard from Uncle Corey."

"And this is something you thought I should know?"

"He seems to think he found someone who knows who killed Mom and Dad."

"That would be Sokolov. They're in the same prison."

"I mean the one who hired Sokolov."

"Who?"

"He wouldn't tell me; said he wants to tell you and only you."

"He wants me to get him out of prison," Lindsay scoffed.

"If he gives us who killed Mom and Dad, wouldn't that be a fair trade?"

"If he really has something, maybe."

"You have another lead?"

Lindsay didn't bother answering. Instead, she said, "I'm currently suspended. I'm not really an FBI agent at the moment."

"Then get unsuspended. This is Mom and Dad I'm talking about."

Liam ended the call.

Lindsay wasn't sure what to believe when it came to Uncle Corey, but she found herself believing Liam about the bank jobs. That didn't change the fact there was something more going on than a couple of robberies.

She had a bad feeling whatever this was it was far from over.

∞

Continue reading Lindsay Lane's thrilling adventure in the next book – Not Quite The Truth

Review This Book

Thank you so much for reading my book! Your support means everything to me.

If you enjoyed it, I'd love for you to help out the next reader by leaving a quick review. Your insights can make a real difference in helping others decide if this book is right for them. I truly appreciate it, and I'm sure future readers will too!

Please leave a review on Amazon, BookBub, or Goodreads.

Nora Kane

About The Author

Nora Kane may have grown up with friends who were into steamy romance novels, but she was always more interested in the juicy mysteries of Nancy Drew and Agatha Christie. While her friends swooned over Fabio, she was busy trying to solve whodunit.

Fast forward to adulthood, and Nora decided to put her mystery-solving skills to good use by spinning her own thrilling tales of suspense.

She now lives in Pennsylvania with her husband and two daughters, where she fuels her creativity with a daily dose of Bulletproof Coffee (because who needs regular coffee when you're solving crimes?) and a glass of Malbec (because even detectives need to unwind).

When she's not busy crafting page-turners, Nora loves to travel and meet new people. Who knows, maybe she'll find inspiration for her next mystery in a far-off land or from a new acquaintance. Either way, she's always on the lookout for her next case to crack!

Printed in Great Britain
by Amazon